WILLIAM DONAHEY

ADVENTURES of the TEENIE WEENIES

1920 edition with
more than 60 illustrations
by the author

TABLE OF CONTENS

THE TEENIE WEENIES

Who they are and where they live.

The Teenie Weenies are a very tiny little people. The Teenie Weenie children are about half an inch in height and the older Teenie Weenies are from two and a half to three inches tall. Paddy Pinn is the tallest one and he really is a Teenie Weenie giant, for he stands four inches in his stocking feet.

The little folks are so small that a lead pencil is to them a great log and a clothes pin will keep the tiny fire place burning for some time. A large tea cup would almost hold the entire family and they could go swimming all at once in a wash basin.

A potato will keep the Teenie Weenies supplied for several months, while one grain of rice will make one of the little people a square meal. Two baked lima beans will make a meal for the whole family and a thimbleful of butter will last a week.

The Teenie Weenies are so small that big people would hardly notice them and the little folks have to be careful to keep out of their way.

The Teenie Weenies live in an old shoe. They have built on a kitchen and a roof covers the top of the shoe. An old hat is used by the little people for a school house and quarters for the army. On top of the hat is a tiny bell which is used for a school bell and also as a fire alarm. On the second floor of the hat the army keeps its uniforms and guns and here the little soldiers drill one night every week.

The Teenie Weenies have many tiny tools and they store all these useful things in an old tin can. There is a work bench in the can and here the men make things and mend the furniture. The shoe house in which most of the Teenie Weenies live is quite crowded, so one corner of the tool house has been made into a comfortable home for Paddy Pinn and Gogo.

An old tea pot has been made into a laundry and here the Chinaman and Zip, the Teenie Weenie wild man, live and do the family washing each week. The little folks have made a cigar box into a wonderful hospital and there the Doctor lives.

Mr. and Mrs. Lover have their own home and live, with their two children, who are twins, in a baby shoe which has been made into a beautiful bungalow.

All of these tiny buildings are close to each other under a certain rose bush and there the little folks live happily together.

The Teenie Weenies ask that the place where they live shall not be told, as they are afraid curious folks might come around to see them. "Not that we wouldn't like to have big people visit us," they say, "but, you see, being so little we might get tramped on and that would be quite the end of us."

INTRODUCING THE TEENIE WEENIES

The General is the head of the Teenie Weenie family. He is very kind and wise and all the little folks trust and love him.

The Doctor looks after the health of the Teenie Weenies, and he is often called to help sick birds, mice and squirrels, for his skill as a doctor is known for quite a distance about the rose bush. He has an office in the Teenie Weenie hospital, and there he is able to treat the sick Teenie Weenies in the best possible way.

The Teenie Weenie Cook is boss of the kitchen and he cooks the most wonderful food that any Teenie Weenie ever tasted. His stove is made out of an old tin tobacco can. The oven is so big that a whole stuffed prune can be baked in it.

Gogo, the little colored Teenie Weenie, is the assistant cook and he can get up almost as good a meal as the Cook. The General says that no one can bake a lima bean as well as Gogo.

The Dunce is a foolish fellow, who is always doing funny things. He is always hungry and the Cook says that he can eat a thimbleful of pudding and then get inside the thimble. All the Teenie Weenies love the Dunce, for he is a kind hearted little chap.

The Old Soldier has only one leg but he is a good carpenter and he can make beautiful furniture out of a few matches. He is also a good tailor and he knows how to mend shoes wonderfully.

The Lady of Fashion is the most beautiful Teenie Weenie lady. She dresses in the very latest style and makes many things with her tiny needle. She is house keeper at the shoe house and often helps the Doctor, for she is a good nurse.

The Policeman is a fat little fellow whose duty it is to walk about and look after the Teenie Weenie children. He settles disputes among the Teenie Weenies and chases away bugs that get too near to the Teenie Weenie houses.

Grandpa is the very oldest Teenie Weenie. He is crippled up with rheumatism and spends most of his time sitting in front of the Teenie Weenie fireplace.

The Chinaman looks after the Teenie Weenie washing. He lives in an old tea pot, which has been made into a fine laundry. The spout of the tea pot makes a good chimney, for the Chinaman must have a fire most of the time, as he needs hot water to wash the clothes and also a place to heat his tiny irons.

Zip is the Teenie Weenie wild man. He came from a tribe of tiny wild men to live with the Teenie Weenies. He rooms with the Chinaman and helps with the washing.

The Cowboy is a great mouse-back rider; in fact he can ride most anything. He once rode a bucking grass hopper but he said it was pretty hard work. He can throw the lasso with wonderful skill and he is a good hunter.

The Indian is a silent little fellow. He spends much of his time in the woods and he can follow the trail of a caterpillar in the wildest jungle of tall grass.

The Scotchman is quite a musical Teenie Weenie. He plays the bagpipes and dances many fancy steps.

The Sailor is a great swimmer and knows all about boats.

The Turk is very strong. He can lift a thimble full of water above his head and he can carry a lead pencil on his shoulder. He knows a great deal about machinery, too.

Rufus Rhyme is the Teenie Weenie poet, who writes verse and songs for the rest of the Teenie Weenies to sing.

Paddy Pinn is the tallest Teenie Weenie and he is a very jolly and wise man.

The Clown is a happy-go-lucky fellow, who can walk on his hands and tumble as well as an acrobat. He loves to play jokes and the Dunce is his great chum.

Tessie Bone is the newest Teenie Weenie. She joined the Teenie Weenie family not long ago and all the little people are very fond of her, in spite of the fact that she is quite a tomboy.

There are several Teenie Weenie women and children and all these little people live very contentedly in their tiny houses under the rose bush.

All the Teenie Weenies must do their share of the work. If you don't work you can't eat, is their motto and the work is usually done, for all the little folks have good appetites.

Every day some Teenie Weenie has to help the Cook and Gogo wash up the dishes and the next day he has to help the Lady of Fashion make the beds and sweep up the house, while on another day he must help cut wood for the stoves and the fireplaces.

With all the Teenie Weenies helping it does not take a great while to do the work, so the little people have most of the day to spend as they like.

The Teenie Weenies are always ready to help a friend in need and many times they have helped the squirrels, the birds, the rabbits and the mice, who live near the rose bush.

Every summer the little people plant a garden and raise many vegetables which they store away in a great cellar under a tiny hill near the shoe house.

Each fall the Cook makes delicious jelly and apple butter and puts up many cans of fruit and vegetables for use during the long winter. The little people smoke many fish and frog hams too.

Four potatoes will keep the Teenie Weenie family supplied all winter and when the Cook wants some potatoes for a meal he goes into the cellar and cuts off a piece. He then covers the place on the potato where he has cut out the piece with hot paraffine and in this manner he keeps the potato in good shape until it is used up.

Apples, carrots, and beets are kept in the same way, so you see the Teenie Weenies have plenty to eat during the winter.

In the summer they live on fresh fruit and vegetables from their garden, while once a week they buy a fresh minnow from a friendly King Fisher for a fish dinner. Occasionally they buy an egg from an old hen, which keeps them supplied with food for a long time, but the Teenie Weenies don't have eggs often, for they are expensive, as the old hens demand twenty-five grains of corn for each egg.

THE EASTER EGG

Humpty Dumpty sat on a hill,
Humpty Dumpty had a great spill;
All the Teenies, ladies and men,
Can't put Humpty Dumpty together again.

Rufus Rhyme, Teenie Weenie Poet.

"WELL, madam," said the General, lifting his hat and bowing politely to the old hen who lived near the shoe house, "will it be possible for you to furnish the Teenie Weenies with an egg for their Easter dinner this year?"

"Why, yes, of course," snapped the old hen. "Ain't I always ready to lay an egg when I gets my pay?"

"Dear me," whispered the Lady of Fashion to the Doctor, "did you ever in all your life hear such bad grammar?"

"How much will you charge us?" asked the General, as he sat down on a pebble.

"Twenty-five grains of corn," answered the hen, glaring about at the Teenie Weenies.

"Great guns!" exclaimed the General, "why, that's five bags, and last year we paid you only three."

"Things are awfully high now and worms are scarce; well, all right, you can have an egg for twenty grains of corn, and not one grain less," cried the old hen.

"That's pretty expensive," said the General, "but it wouldn't seem like Easter if we didn't have a boiled egg, so I'll take it and we'll bring over the corn in the morning and get the egg."

The next morning the little folks filled four teenie weenie bags with corn. Five grains were put into each bag and it was about all a Teenie Weenie could do to carry it.

When the Teenie Weenies arrived at the hen's house they opened the bags and poured the corn out on the ground so the old hen could count them, for she was a businesslike old lady and wanted to be sure that she was getting her full amount of corn.

"I'm not afraid you'll cheat me," she said, "but any one is liable to make a mistake and I always believe in being careful in a business deal."

"That's right, that's right," said a big rooster with a huge double chin, who strutted up to the hen house. "You can't be too careful when it's a matter of business."

"How are you going to get the egg home?" asked the old hen.

"Oh we can roll it very nicely," answered the General.

"Well, I was just going to say that I couldn't deliver it at the low price of twenty grains of corn," cackled the hen. "Give me ten grains more and I'll walk over to the shoe house and lay it anywhere you say."

"It isn't far and we can roll it easily," answered the General.

"Well clear out and give me a little time and I'll lay the egg for you," said the hen. "You don't think I can lay an egg with all you folks standin' around here starin', do you?"

The Teenie Weenies retired to the other end of the chicken yard, where they sat down on several corn cobs to wait.

Presently the old hen announced the laying of the egg with loud cackles and the little folks started at once to roll the egg home.

It was easy work rolling the egg over the level ground, but when the Teenie Weenies came to a steep hill that lay in their path they found that it would be necessary to use ropes in order to let it down safely. The little fellows rolled the egg up to the edge of the hill, while the Turk made the ropes ready to handle the heavy load.

Suddenly a puff of wind struck the egg and it rolled over the edge of the hill. The Cook and Gogo tried to catch it, but they were too late, and the egg and the two Teenie Weenies tumbled down the hill. The Policeman, who was standing below, just had time to fall out of the way as the egg and the Cook rolled past him and smashed up against an old birch.

The Cook was able to save a great deal of the broken egg, which he dipped up into many wash tubs and thimbles. The Teenie Weenies went to bed that night with heavy hearts, for they knew that it would be quite impossible to buy another egg at such high prices.

Easter morning Shoehurst was filled with the greatest excitement, for on the ground in front of the house lay a fine big egg. Most of the Teenie Weenies thought the Easter rabbit had left the egg, but they were greatly mistaken, for the old hen, who was really a kind-hearted old lady in spite of her gruff manner, had heard of the broken egg and, feeling sorry for the little people, had slipped over early in the morning and laid the egg herself.

THE RAIN CAME DOWN BY THE THIMBLEFUL

WHEN Zip, the little wild man, came to live with the Teenie Weenies there wasn't a bit of room left in the old shoe house, so the kind hearted Chinaman took the little chap into his tea pot laundry. There was plenty of room in the old tea pot, so here the two little fellows lived in great comfort and Zip paid for his board by helping the Chinaman launder the Teenie Weenie clothes.

Zip and the Chinaman had eaten a great deal of the easter egg and being tired and sleepy they had retired quite early. While the little chaps lay dreaming in their tiny beds, a great storm came up and the big rain drops came down by the thimbleful. The little men were awakened by the roar of the rain drops splashing on the roof, but they merely turned over in their beds and went to sleep again, for why should they worry about the storm when they were sheltered in a strong tea pot?

Presently the Chinaman was awakened by a queer bouncing of his bed, and to his great astonishment he found that he was floating about the room. The frightened Chinaman sat straight up, and as he did so he lost his balance and tumbled kersplash into the water. He quickly jumped to his feet and found that the water was just up to his waist. Next he groped about the room for some Teenie Weenie matches and in a few minutes he lit a tiny candle.

A wonderful sight met the little fellow's eyes, for all about the room chairs, tables, and things floated in great confusion. Zip lay snoring on his bed, which floated about, and the Chinaman had to shake him hard before he could be awakened.

"Zippie! Zippie! klick! klick!" shouted the Chinaman. "Wake up klick! Oh, suchee muchee wet."

Poor Zip was scared half out of his wits when he looked about the room and it didn't take the two Teenie Weenies long to grab a few clothes and scramble up onto the roof, for the water was almost up to their necks and was rising fast. The rain had stopped, but it was pitch dark, so the little fellows could do nothing but put on their clothes and wait for daylight.

The rest of the Teenie Weenie houses were not injured by the heavy rain, for they stood on the high ground and the water ran off down the hill into the little hollow in which the tea pot stood. The laundry was entirely surrounded by water, which was fully fourteen Teenie Weenie feet deep, and as neither of the little men dared swim among the floating sticks, they were forced to wait until help arrived.

Shortly after daylight the Chinaman and Zip were discovered sitting on top of the tea pot and in a short time the Teenie Weenies came to their rescue. They made a raft out of a couple of clothes pins, an old lead pencil and some boards. Gogo and the Turk pushed the raft through the floating rubbish about the tea pot and soon landed the Chinaman and Zip on dry land.

"J-J-J-Jimminie fish hooks!" exclaimed the Dunce, who was much excited over the rescue. "When I-I-Ig-g-go to bed to-night I'm goin' to take a c-c-c-cork with me for a life preserver."

"Allee same me savee irons," cried the Chinaman, who had brought two of his flat irons through the flood.

"It's a mighty good thing you held onto those irons," laughed the Clown. "They might have floated away."

The ground around the laundry was a sight when the water finally settled, for the Teenie Weenie wood pile was quite near and pencils, matches, and many sticks lay scattered all over the ground.

The Teenie Weenies carried eight thimblefuls of mud out of the tea pot and in a short time the little folks had the laundry as clean as a billiard ball, for every one of the little people helped with all his might.

GOGO AND THE COOK RUN ACROSS AN EARLY BIRD

A FEW days after the big flood, Gogo and the Cook washed up the breakfast dishes, cleaned the kitchen and set out in search of a mushroom for lunch.

"There's some powerful big fat ones over in de big field," remarked Gogo. "Why dere was one we all saw one day what was so big that fo' of us done stand under it while it was rainin' and nevah a single drop done touch us."

"Listen," whispered the Cook as the little fellows were making their way through some tall grass, "what in the name of goodness is that awful noise?"

"Sounds powerful funny like," answered Gogo. "Suppose we go through the weeds and see what it is." The two Teenie Weenies pushed their way quietly through the thick weeds and soon they saw a sight which made them laugh. A young robin stood at the side of a freshly spaded flower bed, and in his beak he held one end of a big, fat worm. The other end of the worm was fast in a piece of earth and the robin, with his feet braced, was holding on to the worm with all his might. The robin was gurgling and trying to call for help through his half closed beak, and the two Teenie Weenies quickly saw he needed help if he wished to save the worm.

"Hold on tight!" shouted the Cook, running up to the bird, "and we'll get a pick and dig this old worm out for you."

The bird nodded his head, while the two little chaps hurried over to the shoe house, where they secured a pick and shouted to the rest of the Teenie Weenies to follow.

The Turk caught hold of the bird's tail and helped him hold on to the worm, while the Dunce pushed on the robin's chest with all his strength. Gogo soon broke the piece of earth up with the pick and with one gulp the robin swallowed the worm.

"Whee!" exclaimed the bird, as he moved his head around to ease the stiffened muscles. "That was some hard job. I haven't worked as hard as that for my breakfast for a long time.

"I saw that worm and I grabbed onto him, but he was a strong old fellow, for he certainly did hang onto that piece of earth with a powerful grip. I hung right onto him, for I hadn't had a worm for several days, and I made up my mind I'd have him if I had to hold on all day."

"Well, you certainly got him, all right!" laughed the Policeman.

"You bet I did, thanks to your help," grinned the bird.

"How would you all like to hear a verse?" said the Poet, who had been writing on a piece of tiny paper while the Teenie Weenies had been helping the bird to get the worm.

"We'd like to hear it!" shouted the Teenie Weenies.

"This verse is entitled 'Would You,'" said the Poet, as he stepped onto a piece of earth in full view of the little people:

"I'd love to be a little bird and hop about the trees,
And aeroplane above the land and fly across the seas.
I wouldn't like to eat the things that little birdies do,
For I don't care a bit for worms, now honestly, do you?"

THE DUNCE PICKS A SOFT PLACE TO FALL

EVERY Sunday afternoon, when the weather was pleasant, the Teenie Weenies took a long walk. "It's good for your health," the General told them, "and, besides, it's a good way to put in the Sabbath afternoon."

One Sunday while they were out on their walk they stopped near a house to chat a bit with a couple of sparrows, and as the little party talked the General happened to see the Dunce crawl up a vine onto a window sill and disappear through the open window.

"Mr. Policeman," said the General, "I wish you would follow that foolish Dunce and see what he is up to."

The Policeman quickly followed the Dunce through the window, but presently he appeared on the sill and motioned the General to come up. The General climbed the vine, followed by the rest of the Teenie Weenies, and crossing over to the inside of the window sill he saw a most alarming thing. Right below him stood a table and on the table stood the Dunce, almost knee deep in a piece of custard pie.

"Well, sir," cried the General sternly, while the rest of the Teenie Weenies tried to keep from laughing, "haven't I told you not to meddle with things when you go into people's houses? What do you mean by disobeying me this way?"

"J-J-J-Just a minute, G-G-G-General, and I'll explain," shouted the Dunce, waving his dripping hands at the General. "It's all an accident, you see, and this is the way it-it-it all happened. While you all were down there talking to those sparrows I happened to see this window was open and I thought I'd climb down here on the table, and j-j-just then I-I-I-somethin' told me I-I-I was about to have a fall, and—and as long as I had to have a fall I thought I might just as well fall into the pie. You see, it being a custard pie, I knew that it was s-s-soft, and, of course I wanted to fall onto somethin' soft. Why, it almost scares me to death when I stop to think that if that pie had been an apple pie, with a-a-a hard crust on it, I might have broken an arm or somethin'.

"Well when I found I was goin' to fall I stepped up to the edge of the window sill, just above the pie, for I wanted to fall into something soft When I landed in the pie I made up my mind that it wouldn't hurt anything if I took a bite, so I-I-I-I took a lick or two."

"Well, sir," said the General, "I have a feeling that I'm going to fall, and I believe that as long as I've got to fall it might as well be on you."

"Wh-wh-what do you mean, General?" asked the frightened Dunce.

"I mean, sir," growled the General, "that I saw a toothpick outside on the ground, and I'm going to get it and give you a much deserved whipping."

The Dunce slowly crawled out of the pie, climbed to the window sill and followed the General down the vine to the ground.

The General picked up half a tooth pick, which lay on the ground, and taking the naughty fellow by the arm he led him back of an old tin bucket.

"Now sir," said the General sadly. "This is going to hurt me more than it will hurt you."

"I-I-I'll t-t-trade places with you, G-G-General," stuttered the Dunce.

The General was a most kind hearted little man and he seldom used the switch, but the Dunce had been warned many times to keep from meddling, and he had to be punished.

He struck the Dunce several times very lightly across his teenie weenie legs and the little chap yelled as though he was being killed.

It didn't hurt the Dunce a bit and he simply yelled because he was frightened, but it did him a great deal of good, for he behaved himself for a long time, which goes to show that even a Teenie Weenie needs a teenie weenie bit of punishment once in a while.

HELP! POLICEMANS!

"THUNDERIN' SNAILS!" exclaimed Paddy Pinn, shortly after the little folks had helped the robin get his breakfast, as he picked up one of the tiny garden hoes the Teenie Weenies use. "I'd bust this hoe with one dig, that's what I'd do," and the big fellow burst out in a loud laugh.

"Well, that's the best we've got to offer you," said the Old Soldier.

"I'll make one for myself before a grasshopper can shake his left hind foot, that's what I'll do," cried Paddy, and he ran off towards the rose bush under which the Teenie Weenies lived. In a few minutes he returned with a big thorn, which he had cut from a dead brier, and, using a match for a handle, he made a fine hoe by tying the thorn to the match.

"There!" he exclaimed holding it up. "That's what I call a man's sized hoe, that's what I do."

The little people set out for the garden, as the General had ordered them to hoe the lima beans. A number of seeds had been planted, for the Teenie Weenies were fond of lima beans and they usually had to store away about two hundred and fifty beans to last them through the winter.

"It will take quite a few more beans this winter," said the General, "for our family is larger now."

"Why the Dunce can eat twenty himself," laughed the Cook.

"You bet I could," cried the Dunce, who was always hungry. "I could eat a whole lima bean right this minute."

"Why you couldn't eat half a bean at once," said the Old Soldier.

"Well, I bet a grape seed I could eat a third of a bean, anyhow," answered the Dunce.

The Teenie Weenie garden was hidden away where grown-up people would not be likely to tramp on the plants and as the little folks trudged along Gogo struck up the following song, while all the rest joined in the chorus:

"Beans they take the place of meat,
And so if we all wish to eat,
We must take our rake and hoe
And scratch the earth to make 'em grow.

CHORUS
"Hoe, hoe, rake and hoe!
Digging up and down the row.
Hoe, hoe, rake and hoe!
If you want to see them grow."

The Teenie Weenies soon arrived at the garden and they set to work at once, still singing the little song and keeping time with the music as their tiny hoes struck the ground.

The Lady of Fashion helped with the work, but she was very careful not to soil her new garden suit, especially her tiny boots, which were made out of the finest frog leather.

"Listen!" said the Old Soldier, "I thought I he—" But he did not finish the sentence, for loud screams came from the tall grass back of the garden.

"Helpee! Helpee! Policemans, policemans!" came a voice, and suddenly the frightened Chinaman burst into sight with the most alarming speed.

Hanging onto his shirt tail was a big fat pinching-bug and the scared Chinaman was only touching the ground about every six inches.

Paddy Pinn struck the bug on the head with his huge hoe, as the Chinaman went by, and it rolled over on the ground half stunned by the mighty blow.

"Where did you pick up your friend," asked the General, as he watched the bug scurry away through the tall grass.

"Me no pickee him up," gasped the Chinaman. "Allee same he pick me up. Me sit down under bush to rest and me go sleepee. Me wakee up much klick and, whillikers, me see blig plinch bug and me run, but he catchee to shirtee tail and me runnee like glasshopper!"

"I should say you did run like a grasshopper," laughed the Cowboy.

"Allee same you run like glasshopper, too," glared the Chinaman, "if blig plinchin'-bug was hangin' on your shirtee tail."

FUZZY-WUZZY

THE Dunce teased the Chinaman a great deal after his experience with the pinching-bug, but the little fellow took it in good humor.

"Allee same me havee chance to laughee at you sometime maybe," said the Chinaman. "Me no get mad but me likee chance to laugh at you."

"All right Chink," laughed the Dunce, "if I ever get a pinchin'-bug on my shirt tail you can laugh yourself sore."

"Well me waitee; maybe time come when me allee same laughee," said the Chinaman.

The Chinaman's chance came sooner than he expected. Every Sunday afternoon the Teenie Weenies took a long walk, for it was healthful to walk in the fresh air, and besides it made them hungry for the fine dinner which the Cook always prepared.

One Sunday during their walk the little people stopped to pay a short call on an old hen and her chickens who lived some little distance from the shoe house. After chatting with the hen and her children for some time the little people continued their walk through a big open field where they finally sat down to rest on a soft, mossy bank.

"Where's the Dunce?" asked the General, as he sat down beside the Lady of Fashion.

"I haven't seen him since we left the old hen," answered the little lady.

"He's back there teasing those chickens," announced Gogo. "I told him he'd better look out, or the first thing he knew he'd get a powerful good peckin', for one of them fuzzy chickens looked mighty mad, that's what she did."

"It would just serve him right," laughed the General. "And maybe it would teach him a lesson—"

"H-e-l-p! H-e-l-p!" came a voice from over a bank of earth, and suddenly the Dunce dashed into view followed by a very angry young chicken. The frightened Dunce was covering the ground in great leaps and just as he ran into the midst of the startled Teenie Weenies the chicken overtook him.

"There, you little rascal!" shouted the chicken, giving the Dunce a peck with her beak which sent the little chap sprawling in the dirt.

"What's the trouble?" asked the General, jumping to his feet.

"He was callin' me 'fuzzy-wuzzy' and throwing things at me—that's what he was," said the chicken, "and I stood it just as long as I could and I chased him, that's what I did, and I'll do it again, too, if he ever teases me again."

"You did exactly the right thing," said the General, "and I hope this will be a lesson to him."

"I suppose I shouldn't have lost my temper, but I couldn't stand it another minute," said the chicken as she trotted away in the direction of her home.

"J-J-J-Jimminie C-C-C-Christmas!" exclaimed the Dunce, "but that fool chicken gave me an awful wallop."

That night there was a big black and blue spot on the Dunce's back and the Doctor had to rub it with salve, but it really did the foolish fellow a lot of good, for he has done no teasing since.

THE CHINAMAN ASKS FOR A CISTERN

"WELL Chink, what can I do for you this morning?" asked the General, as the Chinaman took off his hat and stepped into the Teenie Weenie library.

"Allee same me gottee flavor me want to ask," said the little fellow.

"Sit down, sir, and tell me what it is," smiled the General, pushing a tiny chair towards the Chinaman.

"Well," said the Chinaman, "me gottee lot of washie allee time and me use lottee water."

"Yes, I imagine you use a lot of water."

"Oh yes!" exclaimed the Chinaman. "Me use muchee much. Sometimes me use ten, twenty, twenty-three thimblefuls when me have bigwash. Me likee water from roof, it muchee much better to washee clothes in, but when the rain he no come down me have to carry water from cleek and that long way to carry wash water."

"Yes it is," agreed the General, "and we will have to build a cistern so you can have all the water you need without having to carry it so far."

"Yes me wantee clistern; me need clistern and me likee vlery much to have clistern."

"You shall have a cistern. I'll give orders for one to be built right away," said the General.

The General went out in search of the Old Soldier, who was cutting some matches up for fire wood, and the two Teenie Weenies discussed the matter of a cistern for some time.

"We ought to have a good big cistern," said the Old Soldier, "and I believe that we could make a good one by sinking a tin can in the ground."

After a great deal of talk about the matter the little men decided to build the cistern as near the center of the little village as possible.

"You see," said the Old Soldier, "if we build it at some central point we won't have to lay so many pipes, and we will be able to catch all the water from most of the roofs."

The next morning the little people went to work, and, while several of the Teenie Weenies dug a deep hole near the shoe house, the rest went out in search of a tin can to fill the hole.

On an ash heap not far away they found an old tin can and after a great deal of labor the little folks rolled it up to the hole. When the hole had been dug deep enough the Teenie Weenies rolled it in and then filled the earth in around the edges, so that when the work was done only the top could be seen.

The Teenie Weenies used dried hollow reeds for water pipes and when they had been painted thoroughly with a water proof paint, which the Old Soldier boiled up in a thimble, they carried the water nicely.

The pipes were connected up with the spouting from the tiny roofs and laid in trenches to the cistern. The top of the can was cut off and a tight fitting cover was put on. A little door was left in the top of the cover, so a bucket could be lowered and water drawn up when it was needed. A bucket made out of a hazel nut was used for the purpose, and it took three buckets full to fill a thimble.

"Now allee we need is a rain," cried the Chinaman, when the work was finished. "And me hope it rainee like everythings to-night."

"Well you may have your wish, Chink," said the Sailor, looking up at the sky. "It sort of looks like we may have a shower to-night."

The Sailor was right. It did rain that night and it rained hard.

The Chinaman was up at daylight to see whether the cistern had been filled, and to the great joy of the little chap he found it full to the very top.

THE DOCTOR SAVES A BIRD

"DOCTOR!" shouted the Dunce one morning, as he popped his head into the library, "t-t-there's a b-b-bird outs-s-side who wants to s-s-see you."

"All right," answered the Doctor, "tell him I'll be out in a minute."

"I think he's a her," said the Dunce, "but anyhow she's awfully excited and I think something terrible must have happened."

The Doctor stepped out onto the Teenie Weenie front porch, and before the house he saw a bird in the act of shaking a tear off the end of her bill.

"Well, madam," said the Doctor, "what can I do for you?"

"Oh, Doctor," cried the bird, "please save my baby! I have lost two babies in the last month and please, oh, please, save my last baby for me."

"Be calm, my dear lady," said the Doctor, "and tell me all about the case."

"Well," began the mother, "I had three lovely babies this spring and about six weeks ago two of them were taken suddenly ill. I did everything I could for them, but they both died and only last night my last baby was taken sick. A squirrel, who lives in a tree near my nest, told me about you and I decided to come to you for help."

"I'll get my medicine case and join you in a minute," said the Doctor, and running into the tiny house he soon returned.

"Jump right onto my back," said the bird, "and I'll take you to my baby in a jiffy."

The Doctor climbed onto the bird's back and in another minute he found himself sailing over the tops of the trees so fast he could scarcely breathe. In a few minutes the bird landed on a bush and quickly hopped to a pretty nest hidden beneath the green leaves. The Doctor slid off into the nest, where he found a young and very sick bird.

"Let's see your tongue," said the Doctor, but the poor bird was so sick he could hardly open his mouth and the Doctor was forced to take hold of his beak and help. Next the Doctor examined the bird's eyes and felt his pulse.

"What has the patient been eating lately?" asked the Doctor.

"I have given him only the nicest and fattest bugs and worms I could find," answered the mother.

"Madam," said the Doctor, "your baby is a very sick boy, but I think I can save his life if you will follow my advice."

"I'll do anything to save my boy," cried the poor mother.

"First," said the Doctor, "the patient must not have much to eat. He will have to have a special diet, which the Teenie Weenie Cook will prepare for him. The patient must be kept dry at all costs," continued the Doctor.

"I never leave the nest when it's raining," cried the mother bird, "and I keep him just as dry as can be."

"You keep the rain off your child, no doubt," said the Doctor, "but the nest gets wet and it must be kept dry too."

The bird carried the Doctor back to the shoe house, where he soon made arrangements for taking care of the sick child.

The Teenie Weenies carried boards over to the tree and pulled them up to the nest with ropes and pulleys. They built a strong frame work over the nest and roofed it with card-board, which was given several coats of water proof paint.

"This roof will keep the nest dry," said the Doctor, when the work had been done, "and that is a most important matter."

The Cook made angle-worm broth for the sick bird and he cooked corn and rice in such a delicious way that the poor patient soon began to improve. At the end of a week the bird was much better and three weeks later he was entirely cured.

FRIDAY THE THIRTEENTH

"DO YOU all know what day this is?" asked Gogo, as he stopped at the laundry door and looked mournfully in at the Chinaman, who was singing loudly as he rubbed a tiny shirt up and down his wash board.

"Why allee same it Fliday," answered the Chinaman. "Yes sir," said the little colored Teenie Weenie sadly, "it's mo' than just Friday. It's Friday the thirteenth."

"Allee same what difference?" asked the Chinaman.

"When Friday comes on the thirteenth of the month it's mighty unlucky," answered Gogo, with a most serious expression on his black little face. "You all better look out, 'cause somethin' always happens that is powerful unlucky on a day like this."

"Nothing happen unlucky to me," cried the Chinaman. "Me vely happy. Me gottee clistern full of water and me gottee lottee wash to do, so me too busy to be unlucky," and the little chap began washing all the harder.

"Well just you remembah that I-all told you it was unlucky. I just wanted to wa'n you, dat's all," and Gogo mournfully made his way to the Lovers' bungalow, where he left much advice to Mr. and Mrs. Lover.

Gogo spent most of the morning explaining that it was Friday the thirteenth, and he warned each and every Teenie Weenie that it was a most unlucky day.

"Well Gogo," said the General, when the little people sat down to their noonday meal, "has anything unlucky happened yet?"

"No sir, not yet," answered the little fellow, "but there's plenty o time yet for somethin' to happen. Just you wait and see."

"General," said the Cook, popping his head through the kitchen door, "there isn't a bit of sugar in the house. Every last speck has been used and we haven't a grain."

"Great pinhead!" exclaimed the General, "that's terrible. We can't get along without sugar."

"Didn't I-all tell you dat this was a unlucky day," cried Gogo, looking around at his friends.

"Well it certainly is unlucky if we haven't any sugar in the house," cried the Dunce, who had a large sweet tooth.

"After dinner I'll see what we can do, Cook," said the General. "We certainly must have some sugar."

The Teenie Weenies made their own sugar from the sap of the maple tree, or from the blossoms of sweet clover, but the frost had stopped the flow of the maple sap and the little folks had only been able to make a small amount of sugar.

"It will be quite a spell before we can make sugar out of the sweet clover blossoms," said the Old Soldier, "and we will have to get sugar some other way."

That afternoon the General ordered the Teenie Weenies to go out in search of sugar. "But mind," warned the General, "I don't want any one to take sugar from the big houses unless you see that it is going to waste."

All afternoon the little people searched about the big house, but not one bit of sugar could they find, and as it was growing dark, it began to look as though the Teenie Weenie sugar bowl would be empty that night at supper.

"Dat's all on account of Friday the thirteenth," moaned Gogo. "Dis is suttinly a most unlucky day."

"G-G-General, G-G-G-General," gasped the Dunce as he dashed into the Teenie Weenie sitting room, "Jimminie f-f-f-fishhooks! I found a great big lot of sugar!"

"Where?" asked the excited Teenie Weenies.

"Well," said the Dunce, "I was hurrying along the walk over by the big fence and I saw a little boy stub his toe and fall down. When he got up and went away I went over where he had fallen and I found a bag of sugar. He dropped it when he fell and it was spilled over the sidewalk."

"Didn't he try and pick it up?" asked the Doctor.

"N-N-N-No," answered the Dunce. "He just got up and went on his way."

"Well we certainly can't let that sugar lie there and spoil," smiled the General, and he ordered the Teenie Weenies to rescue as much of the sugar as possible.

Taking shovels and thimbles the little folks hurried to the bag of sugar, where they set to work carrying it to their store house.

They worked until it was quite dark and when the last bit of sugar which could be saved had been carried to the store room, it filled an old teacup.

It took eighty-four thimblefuls to fill the cup and the Cook announced that it would be quite enough to last the little family through the canning season.

"Well Gogo," said the Old Soldier, as the little people sat around the tiny fire place after dinner, "considerin' that cupful of sugar we found today, Friday the thirteenth hasn't proved so very unlucky."

"N-N-N-No, taint," answered the little fellow sadly, "but it's been mighty unlucky for that little boy that stubbed his toe, just the same."

AN INVITATION

"SAY Cook," said the Dunce, peering into the Teenie Weenie kitchen, "can't we make s-s-some t-t-taffy? You have a lot of sugar now and I thought maybe you could s-s-s-spare s-s-s-some."

"Oh, I suppose so!" answered the Cook. "But just remember this; I don't want you to get things mussed up, and you've got to clean the kitchen up when you're through."

"Yes s-s-sir, we will," cried the Dunce, and he hurried out to tell the good news to the Clown. But as he ran out of the door all thoughts of taffy popped from his tiny head, for he saw a most unusual sight.

Up the walk came six Teenie Weenies staggering under the weight of a big letter and it was addressed to the Teenie Weenies.

The little men dropped the letter on the ground before the shoe house and quickly cut the envelope open with one of their tiny axes.

A piece of paper was folded inside the envelope and the little people soon pulled it out and spread it on the ground.

"Read it, General, read it!" shouted the excited Teenie Weenies.

"All right," cried the General; "keep quiet and I'll read it aloud."

The little folks had been chattering like a lot of magpies, but they instantly held their tiny tongues and gathered closely about the edge of the letter.

"Dear Teenie Weenies," began the General, "I thought I would write to you and ask you if you would come and live in my doll house. I have a nice doll house and it would make a very nice place for you to live in. I will cook good things for you to eat. You can play with my toys and I have a little toy horse that the Dunce can ride on.

"You can have a pan of water to swim in. I will make beautiful clothes for the Lady of Fashion. I will make cookies for you, and I will make candy too. Please come. I would like to have you come.

"Yours truly, your friend, Helen Meyers."

"J-J-J-Jimminie f-f-f-fishhooks!" shouted the Dunce, "let's go. I can pack my suit case in two shakes of a grasshopper's hind leg."

"Why goodness sakes!" exclaimed the Lady of Fashion, who had been looking at the little girl's address at the bottom of the letter. "This little girl lives quite near and we could go over to her house and see her doll house."

"Let's do it," shouted the little people so earnestly that the General gave his consent and they set off immediately.

After a long walk the Teenie Weenies finally arrived at the little girl's home and, finding the coast clear, they soon made their way into the house.

In the corner of a room the little folks found the doll house, which they examined from top to bottom.

"Well, it's a nice enough house to look at," remarked the Cook, as he stepped out onto the front porch, "but there isn't any running water or a sink in the kitchen."

"And there isn't a bath room," cried the Lady of Fashion. "I simply couldn't live in a house that had no bath."

"That just suits me," said the Dunce, who hated baths.

"It's built out of paper," said the Old Soldier. "I'd never live in a house that was built out of paper. There's too much danger of fire and besides no insurance company would ever insure a paper house," and the Old Soldier sat down on the little porch.

"Well," said the General, sitting down beside the Old Soldier, "I don't think we want to give up the old shoe house. Even if it is old, it's a pretty comfortable place after all." And all the little folks quite agreed with him.

The Teenie Weenies were much interested in the little girl's doll, which sat near the doll house, and they examined it very carefully. Of course the Dunce had to climb all over the doll, although the Policeman had warned him to keep off. Finally he got his feet tangled in the doll's hair and fell off its head right on top of the Policeman, who was so angry that he marched the Dunce home, and sent him to bed with nothing to eat but water and bread.

The little girl never knew that the Teenie Weenies had paid her a visit, but had she examined the front porch of her doll's house she might have seen tiny foot prints in the dust.

The next morning the Teenie Weenies answered the little girl's letter and here it is, just as the little people set it down:

"Dear Helen:

"We want to thank you for your kind invitation, but we think it would be much better for us to live in the old shoe house. Shoehurst is quite comfortable, and it is so pretty under the old rose bush we should hate to give it up. The big briars, with their sharp thorns, guard us like a sentinel and keep big feet from treading on our home, and in the summer the cool leaves shield us from the hot sun. It is beautiful in June, when the scent of roses is in the air, to lie on the cool moss and listen to the humming of the bees.

"Your kind invitation has given us a great deal of pleasure, for it's mighty nice to know that people want us to come and live with them, even if we can't do it.

"We can't leave Shoehurst, for, although it's nothing but an old shoe, it's home.

"Again thanking you for your generous invitation, we are, sincerely yours,

"The Teenie Weenies."

THE MOUSE-BACK RACE

ALTHOUGH the Teenie Weenies refused to live with big people, they never tired of going into the big houses, for there were many wonderful things to see in them.

"It was mighty nice of that little girl to ask us to come and live in her doll's house," said the Old Soldier, "but if we lived all the time in a big house we'd get so used to them we wouldn't care to visit them and that would spoil a lot of our fun, for it really is a great pleasure to wander among the things that big people use."

One afternoon several of the little folks were taking a walk when they stopped before a big house.

"Let's go in and look around," said the Dunce, who had fond hopes of finding something good to eat.

"Allee same this house where Blillie Mouse lives," cried the Chinaman.

"That's so," said the General. "Let's go in and make a call on Billie."

"Yes, let's do it," cried the rest of the Teenie Weenies, and they quickly made their way into the cellar where Billie Mouse lived.

The entrance to the home of Mr. Mouse was through a crack between two bricks. The General knocked loudly several times, and receiving no answer, he told the rest to wait for him, and stepped boldly in. He found no one at home, and so, leaving his card, returned to the waiting Teenie Weenies.

"I'm awfully sorry Mr. Mouse is out," said the Lady of Fashion, as the little people moved away. "I haven't seen him for a long time."

"Here he comes now," cried the Cook, pointing toward a pile of lumber at the other end of the cellar. "And there's another mouse with him."

Billie Mouse saw the Teenie Weenies, and came bounding joyfully up to them.

"My, it does my eyes good to see you again," he cried. "It's a long time since I have seen you."

Motioning the other mouse to come up, he introduced him to all the Teenie Weenies.

"I'm delighted to meet you," the new mouse said, making a deep bow.

"Well how have you been?" asked the General, sitting down on the edge of an old scrubbing brush.

"Oh I'm in pretty good shape now," answered Billie Mouse, "but I have had a very bad time of it for the last three weeks. I had a bad case of ptomaine poisoning."

"Ptomaine poisoning!" exclaimed the General. "That's rather serious."

"Yes, I was pretty sick for a time," said the Mouse. "Got hold of some cheese that was tainted."

"You ought to be careful of what you eat," cried the Lady of Fashion. "People are always putting out food which has been poisoned."

"I know it," said Billie Mouse, "especially cheese. I'm always suspicious of cheese, but this piece which made me sick looked perfectly good. I smelled it and carefully tasted it before I ate it and I thought it was all right."

"Let's have a race?" suggested the Cowboy, after the two mice and the Teenie Weenies had talked for some time.

The mice agreed, and a race course was soon chosen. The race was to be run between two long boards, and an old scrubbing brush was brought up for a hurdle at the end of the track. The Cowboy was to ride one mouse and the Dunce, who claimed to be a good rider, the other.

"Now," said the General, "the man who rides down the length of these boards and jumps over the scrubbing brush first will win the race."

40

When all was ready the signal was given and down the track came the mice, as fast as they could run, with the Cowboy and the Dunce sticking tightly to their backs. As the mice drew near the hurdle the Dunce was ahead, and it looked as though he would win the race. But just as the mouse sprang into the air to leap over the brush the Dunce lost his grip, and was tossed into the air. The mouse jumped over the brush, and when the Dunce came down he hit the ground with a great thud.

The Cowboy stuck tightly to his mouse, and leaping gracefully over the brush, he was declared winner.

The Dunce was not hurt by his fall. He joined loudly in the laughter that greeted his tumble, and was the first to start a cheer for the Cowboy.

A WATERMELON FEAST

"SAY, Gogo!" shouted the Dunce one morning as he ran up the steps of the shoe house. "Do you like watermelon?"

"Say, foolish person, what you-all askin' such a silly question fo'?" grinned the happy colored Teenie Weenie. "If there is anything in the whole world I like better than watermelon, it's mo' watermelon."

"Well I-I-I know where there's a great b-b-big piece," shouted the Dunce. "It's over on a table in the big green house and there was a man eatin' some and he said that he couldn't eat any more. I heard him, for I climbed up the morning glory vine at the window and watched him."

"Let's go!" shouted several of the Teenie Weenies.

"Well you'd better not be in a hurry," remarked the General, stepping out onto the front porch. "You all know that it wouldn't be right to help yourselves to that watermelon unless the people who own it were going to throw it away."

"Yes s-s-sir, that's j-j-j-just what they are going to do," stuttered the Dunce. "The man said that he couldn't eat any more and a woman said to leave it right on the table and she would throw it out."

"Well that's different," answered the General, who was fond of melon himself. "Under the circumstances we can go over and have a taste."

It took but a short time for the little people to make their way over to the house and, crawling through the crack under the kitchen door, they saw the red top of the melon on the table. To their delight they saw a great deal had been left.

The Teenie Weenies all are wonderful climbers, and it was a simple matter for the little folks to climb up onto the table. They swarmed onto the melon and ate until they could not hold another bite.

After the little people had eaten all they could hold they amused themselves by playing with the various things they found on the table. The Clown climbed up to the top of a fork, which stuck in the melon, and performed some wonderful acrobatic feats. The small boys took off their shoes and stockings, waded in the juice, and pushed themselves about with toothpicks on the huge seeds, which made fine rafts.

Gogo ate until he nearly burst, and the Doctor found the little fellow sitting on the handle of a knife holding his tiny head.

"What's the matter?" asked the Doctor.

"I's in trouble," he groaned.

"Anything serious?" asked the Doctor.

"Yes, sir," answered the colored Teenie Weenie, pointing to the huge slice of melon. "I's plumb full. Can't eat another bite, and all that watermelon before me!"

"Well that is sort of tough," laughed the Doctor, "but if I were you I'd not let that worry me, for you certainly will be sick if you eat any more."

The Cowboy carried several of the seeds back to the shoe house and stored them away in the tool house.

"I'm going to plant these next summer," he said, "and then we can have a watermelon of our own."

"You'd have a hard time cutting it open," suggested the Old Soldier.

"Gosh!" exclaimed the Cowboy, "I never thought of that, but I suppose we could blast it open with dynamite."

"Just leave that to Gogo," laughed the Doctor. "He will find some way to get into it."

The Teenie Weenies were so full of melon they could not eat a bite of lunch—not even the Dunce—and the Cook had a good rest that day.

Poor Gogo ate more than was good for him. He consumed a piece of melon as big as a hickory nut and the Doctor was up half the night putting teenie weenie hot water bottles on his teenie weenie tummie.

THE DUNCE GETS STUCK IN A PLATE OF TAFFY

SEVERAL days after the watermelon feast the Dunce failed to put in an appearance at the noonday meal. This was rather unusual, for he was always hungry and he generally was the first Teenie Weenie to draw his chair up to the tiny table.

"Where's the Dunce?" asked the General, as he carved a slice from a big strawberry and dropped it onto the Cowboy's waiting plate.

"I haven't seen him for a couple of hours," answered the Policeman.

"Last me see him," grunted the Indian, "him go down garden path to big house."

"Well, I think something must have happened to him, for he is always the first to the dinner table," said the General, anxiously.

"I think so, too," put in the Lady of Fashion, "for he knew we were going to have a strawberry for dinner, and that would bring him, if nothing else did."

"Just as soon as we have finished dinner I think some of us had better go out and look for him," said the General.

So, as soon as the meal was over, the Teenie Weenies started out to search for the Dunce.

The Indian pointed out the house near which he had last seen the Dunce, and crawling under the door the Teenie Weenies began to look all about the place.

"Listen," cried the Cook, as he stepped over a safety pin, "I thought I heard him call."

"Help—h-e-l-p!" came a voice faintly from the next room.

"That's him—that's the Dunce's voice," cried the Sailor, and running through the doorway, they saw the tip of the Dunce's cap bobbing up and down over the top of a sideboard.

Climbing up, the Teenie Weenies found the Dunce standing up to his knees in a plate of sticky taffy!

"I—I—I'm stuck," sobbed the Dunce.

"Yes, we can see you are," said the General, with a smile, as he walked up to the side of the plate.

After a great deal of work the Cowboy and the Turk pulled the Dunce out.

"What were you doing in that taffy?" asked the General, as he led the Dunce up the garden towards the Teenie Weenie house.

"I saw the plate," answered the Dunce, "and I—I—I just went up to get a taste and—and—"

"You got stuck fast," said the General.

"Yes—I did," and the Dunce looked sad and sorry.

"Look here," said the General, "you've got to stop this running away, or I'll send you off to the little girl who wrote us a letter and said that if the Dunce would come and live with her, she would reform him, and make a good boy out of him. I think you need reforming."

"Y-yes," said the Dunce, uncertainly.

"What do you think would have happened to you if we hadn't found you and pulled you out of that taffy?" demanded the General.

The Dunce looked frightened. "Why—why," he answered, "I spec' I would have been et!"

THE GREAT FIELD DAY

THE Teenie Weenies teased the Dunce a great deal after his experience in the taffy plate, and if it hadn't been for an event which soon took place he would have had to stand much more of their joking.

For a long time the Teenie Weenies had thought of holding a field day. Their interest in athletics probably started from the example of the Chinaman, who had become quite expert as a pole vaulter. The little fellow made a vaulting pole out of a dry straw, and with this he could vault over a dandelion with the greatest ease.

"Do you-all know that we could have a field day if we really tried?" asked Gogo one afternoon of a group of the little fellows as they sat watching the Chinaman. "Now there is the Chinaman, who could enter the pole vault, the Turk can run fast and he can jump and I can put the shot. Why, we could have a powerful fine field day."

"And say!" exclaimed Rufus Rhyme. "How's this for a yell:

"Rah! Rah! Rah!
Zip boom Fah!
Teenie Weenie! Teenie Weenie!
Rah! Rah! Rah!"

"That's fine!" shouted the little chaps, and they practiced the yell until they fairly rattled the leaves on the old rose bush.

Everybody was greatly excited over the suggestion for a field day, and for several weeks the little men trained for the great event. A place was chosen on a fine sandy spot near the shoe house where the little people could hold their games in perfect safety. A big board fence stood on one side, while a row of bushes protected them from prying eyes on the other side.

For several days the Old Soldier and the Turk had worked hard getting things ready for the great day. Many hurdles were built out of matches and two long poles were set firmly in the ground for the pole

vault. The Teenie Weenie ladies, led by the Lady of Fashion, found a piece of an old silk necktie, which they cut up and made into many tiny pennants, on which they embroidered the Teenie Weenie monogram.

The day of the great event proved to be warm and pleasant and many tiny records were broken by the little folks. Gogo proved to be the hero of the day. Besides acting as trainer to the athletes, he broke the Teenie Weenie record for the shot put, hurling the B B buck shot forty-two and a half (Teenie Weenie) feet, which is twenty-one and a quarter inches in our measurement. This mighty effort beat the record by two and a half feet, which had been held by Paddy Pinn for several years.

The Turk won the hundred and twenty yard hurdle race, beating the Dunce by two seconds. The Scotchman won the hundred yard dash while the Clown took away the honors in the high jump. The little fellow cleared the match at seven and a half (Teenie Weenie) feet, or three and three-quarters inches.

The Chinaman set a new record for the pole vault.

The little chap cleared the straw at fifteen (Teenie Weenie) feet.

The Teenie Weenies had a most wonderful day, and that night they held a banquet in honor of the occasion. The desks were removed from the floor of the school house, a huge table was brought in and the Cook dished up one of the finest dinners the little people ever ate.

The Dunce ate so much of the big stuffed prune, which was served for dessert, that he had to go to bed, but the rest of the little folks danced until a late hour.

THE DUNCE PULLS A TOOTH

"I'LL just bet you a grape seed I'd have won that hurdle race from the Turk, if I hadn't had a toothache," said the Dunce the day after the field day.

"Why don't you-all have it pulled?" asked Gogo.

"Ah say! Jimminie f-f-f-fishhooks!" exclaimed the Dunce. "That would hurt and I'd rather have the t-t-t-toothache."

The poor Dunce was afraid to mention his toothache to the General for fear he would have the Doctor pull it out. He suffered for some time, but at last he could stand it no longer and one day he decided to ask advice.

"Oh, whillikers! Jimminie fishhooks, ouch!" he howled as he ran into the sitting room of the shoe house.

"Now what's the matter?" asked the General.

"I-I-I-I've got the t-t-t-toothache!" wailed the Dunce, holding his hand over his jaw and dancing about on one foot.

"Well, find the Doctor and get attended to," said the General.

The Dunce found the Doctor, and after he had carefully examined the aching tooth he told the Dunce it would have to be pulled.

"What!" shouted the Dunce. "Jimminie Christmas! I-I-I-I'd rather have the t-t-toothache."

"All right, just as you like," said the Doctor.

"Can't you put something on it to make it quit aching?" asked the Dunce.

"That tooth is in bad condition," said the Doctor, "and the only way to stop it for once and all is to pull it."

"All right, s-s-s-sir," groaned the Dunce, "p-p-p-pull it out."

The Doctor got out a tiny pair of forceps and a glass of water. He then had the Dunce sit in one of the easy chairs and told him to open his mouth.

"S-S-S-Say, Doc," stuttered the frightened Dunce, "i-i-i-is it gonna hurt m-m-m-much?"

"Yes, it will hurt a little."

"S-S-S-Say, Doc, c-c-c-couldn't I pull it myself?"

"I suppose you could," answered the Doctor. "You could tie a thread to it with the other end fixed to a stone and then get up on something high and drop the stone. That would certainly pull it out."

"That's w-w-w-what I'm gonna do," and the Dunce jumped out of the chair and disappeared through the doorway.

The Dunce hunted up Gogo and asked that little fellow's advice about pulling the aching tooth.

"Dere's a fine place over the hill just back of the house," said the little black Teenie Weenie. "Dere's a berry basket and you can done climb up on dat, tie on de stone, and out comes dat toof like a cork out of a bottle."

The two little fellows secured a piece of strong silk thread and, followed by a number of the Teenie Weenies, they hurried to the basket back of the house.

The Dunce and Gogo chose a peach seed for the weight to tie to the end of the thread and after boosting it up onto the basket they climbed up themselves. The thread was fixed tightly to the peach seed and the other end was tied to the offending tooth.

"Now all you got to do is to give dat peach seed a kick and out comes dat toof," said Gogo.

"C-C-C-Crickets!" moaned the Dunce, "I-I-I-I got a kind of sick feelin' in my s-s-s-stomach. I think I'll wait awhile."

For full half an hour the Dunce stood trembling on the edge of the basket while Gogo and the Doctor argued with the foolish fellow to kick off the seed and have it all over.

While the Dunce was talking to the Doctor, Gogo suddenly kicked the seed off the basket and the tooth was jerked out of the Dunce's mouth before he really knew what happened.

"Oh, whillikers! Jimminie crickets! Hallelujah!" shouted the Dunce, dancing up and down with joy, when he realized that the tooth was out. "It's out, it's out! Hallelujah, hallelujah!"

AN ADVENTURE WITH A FROG

"ALLEE same where Clowboy?" gasped the Chinaman, stopping at the back porch of the shoe house, were the Cook sat slicing a grape for lunch.

"I saw him a while ago talking to the Indian," answered the Cook. "They were sitting under that big mushroom on the other side of the house."

"Thankee," and the Chinaman hurried around the corner of the house, puffing like a steam engine.

"Oh there you are," he cried, as he spied the Indian and the Cowboy, lying in the shade of the mushroom. "Allee same me gottee much to tell."

"Well what is it, Chink?" asked the Cowboy.

"Me see big clowflog."

"You mean a big bullfrog," corrected the Cowboy.

"Yes, yes—a bulltoad—bullflog," cried the excited Chinaman. "Him sleep on log at pond. Him snore like everythings. You come and throw lasso over his head and we catchee him."

"You round up the fellows and I'll get my rope," cried the Cowboy, smacking his lips over the thought of delicious baked frog ham.

In a few minutes the Teenie Weenies were on their way towards the pond, which lay back of the woods near the shoe house.

"S-s-sh," warned the Indian, as the little people hurried up to the edge of the pond. "Frog him sleep; don't wake."

The Teenie Weenies sneaked along carefully until they stood quite near the log on which the sleeping frog sat. He was a big green fellow and the Teenie Weenies scarcely breathed for fear they would awaken the frog, and lose him.

Several of the strongest Teenie Weenies held the end of the rope while the Cowboy crawled silently onto the log.

"Now when I drop the noose over the frog's head," whispered the Cowboy, "you fellows jerk the rope and hold on for dear life."

The Cowboy slipped quietly up behind the frog and cleverly tossed the rope over the big fellow's head.

Awakened by the rope falling about his neck, the frog gave a mighty leap towards the water. He was a powerful fellow, and went into the water with a great splash, pulling several of the Teenie Weenies with him.

As the frog disappeared beneath the water the Teenie Weenies swam for shore, where they were pulled up onto the bank by their friends, all sputtering, all soaked to the skin, but unhurt.

When the Teenie Weenies discovered that none of the little folks had been hurt by the ducking, they laughed until the tears ran down their teenie weenie faces.

"Ho, ho, ho!" roared the Poet, as he rolled over on the ground with laughter, "I haven't seen anything so funny as this for a long time."

"It's almost as funny as the time the Dunce fell into the dish of apple sauce," giggled the Lady of Fashion.

"Goodee gracious!" exclaimed the Chinaman, who had been looking on with wide opened eyes, "allee same me didn't know that bull clow—I mean bullflog—him so strong."

"Strong!" cried the Doctor, "I should say they are strong. Why a frog has wonderfully powerful legs. He could kick a Teenie Weenie over an ice cream bucket with one blow of his hind leg."

"I wouldn't mind if one kicked me INTO an ice cream freezer," grinned the Dunce, who was fond of ice cream.

"That 'ol frog reminds me of an old song," said Gogo and as the Teenie Weenies walked back towards the shoe house the little colored chap sang this quaint little song:

"Frog went a-courting and he did ride—
Umm humm!
Frog went a-courting and he did ride,
He wore a pistol by his side—
Umm humm!
He rode up to Miss Mouse's house—
Umm humm!
He rode up to Miss Mouse's house—
Said he 'Miss Mouse will you marry me?'
Umm humm!"

SOMETHING ABOUT A BEAR

IT was a warm, lazy sort of morning, and very few Teenie Weenies were to be seen about the rose bush. Grandpa sat fast asleep in his easy chair on the front porch of the shoe house. Gogo was busily engaged carving a sugar bowl out of a large cherry seed, while several of the little men hacked at the wood pile back of the kitchen.

The Policeman was telling a couple of sparrows how the Dunce howled over his tooth being pulled when the Lady of Fashion touched him on the shoulder.

"I beg your pardon," she said, "but do you know where the General is?"

"He's over at the tool house, ma'am," answered the Policeman, touching his hat.

"Is he busy?" asked the little lady.

"I don't think so, ma'am. He's just watching the Old Soldier and Paddy Pinn, who are tanning a frog hide for shoe leather."

"Would you mind asking him to meet me in the library. I want to see him on a matter of great importance," said the Lady of Fashion.

"With pleasure, ma'am," answered the Policeman, and touching his hat again he set off while the Lady of Fashion returned to the shoe house.

"Well, my dear lady," said the General a few minutes later as he stepped into the Teenie Weenie library where the Lady of Fashion sat waiting, "the Policeman tells me that you want to speak with me."

"Yes, General," answered the little lady, "I have something important I want to talk to you about. I want you to do something for me. Something very nice. Will you?"

"Why, I don't know. What do you want?" asked the head of the Teenie Weenies as he sat down in one of the tiny chairs.

"Well," began the little lady, "while I was out walking yesterday with the Doctor, we went into a house to get warm and while we were there we heard a little girl crying as though her heart would break. The little girl had broken the wheel of her toy bear and I wish you would get the boys to go over and fix it for her. She's a child who hasn't many toys."

"I don't see how we can spare the time just now, for we have eleven clothes pins to split up into stove wood and—but we'll do it anyhow!" said the General, as he saw the tears gathering in the Lady of Fashion's eyes.

"Oh, thank you so much!" and the little lady kissed the General on top of his bald little head.

That afternoon the General and several of the Teenie Weenie men walked over to the house where the little girl lived, and had a look at the broken toy. The bear was a big fellow, and one of the solid wooden wheels on which he moved about was broken in two.

"The axle is broken, too," said the Turk, peering under the board on which the bear stood.

"We'll have to make some long bolts to hold the wheel together," announced the Old Soldier, who had been measuring the broken wheel with his tiny tape-measure.

After a great deal of talk and measuring, the little men hurried back to the shoe house, where they set to work making the bolts and nuts necessary for mending the broken bear.

The next morning the Teenie Weenie workmen set off for the little girl's house, followed by a number of the little people who were curious to see the bear. As the little girl had been taken out for a walk, the coast was clear, and the little men started to work at once, while the rest wandered about examining a doll's house and many other toys which stood about the room.

The Teenie Weenies jacked up the bear, fitted in a lead pencil for an axle, bolted together the broken wheel, and in a short time the little men had made the toy as good as new.

When the little girl came back from her walk and found the mended toy she was very happy, and she wondered many, many times just who had fixed the broken bear.

THE INVENTION

"I'LL bet that little girl has wondered many times how her bear was mended," chuckled the Old Soldier, as he stirred up the fire with a big darning needle which the little folks used for a poker.

"She must consider it quite a mystery," said the Lady of Fashion.

"Speaking of mysteries," cried the Turk, "does anybody know what the Dunce is up to?"

The Dunce had been locking himself up in his room for the last few days, in a most mysterious way. He seemed very important and he refused to answer questions.

"I'll bet he is building something," ventured the Cowboy. "He's been hammering away all day."

"I saw him sneaking along this morning with a cork on his shoulder," said the Cook.

"Well just give him a little time and we'll find out," remarked Grandpa, nodding his head wisely. "He's swelling up so with importance he'll have to tell pretty soon or he will bust."

Grandpa was right, for that very evening the Dunce arose from his chair at the teenie weenie supper table and said: "Ladies and gentlemen, I have just finished a great invention and, if I can find some deep water near by, I will be glad to show you something astonishing."

"Three rousing cheers for Thomas Edison Dunce!" shouted the Clown, and the cheers were given with such a will that the squirrel, who lived near the shoe house, came running over and looked in the window to see what the noise was all about.

As the weather was quite cool, the Teenie Weenies thought it would be wise to try the Dunce's invention indoors. So it was decided to go to the big house across the street, where plenty of water could be found in the bathroom. As soon as breakfast was over the next morning the Teenie Weenies hurried over to the house and climbed up to the washstand. After a lot of hard work they got the faucets turned and filled the bowl with water. The Dunce then took two corks from a big package

59

that the Sailor had helped him carry, and strapped them tightly to his feet.

"Now, ladies and gentlemen," shouted the Dunce, "I will show you how easy it is to walk on water."

Letting himself down into the water by the chain to the stopper, the Dunce stepped bravely out toward the center of the bowl. But—as soon as he let go of the chain he lost his balance and fell over, kersplash, into the water! The corks, being so light, pulled his feet to the top of the water, and kept them there, and if the Turk and the Sailor had not promptly dived in after him the Dunce would probably have been drowned.

"G-G-G-Golly." spluttered the Dunce, as he sat dripping, but safe, on the edge of the bowl, "it d-d-didn't w-wo-work, did it?"

The Teenie Weenies had lots of fun teasing the Dunce about walking on the water, and it was many days before he heard the last of his wonderful invention.

THE GREAT BALL

THERE was some great secret in the air. For some time there had been much stir in and about the Teenie Weenie village beneath the rose bush. There were many secret meetings between the General and the Lady of Fashion, who seemed to be the leading spirits of it all. The Turk and the Cook and Gogo, under the direction of the Lady of Fashion, spent many days in the cellar of a certain house not far from Shoehurst. The Lovers' bungalow was closed to all gentlemen callers every afternoon for several weeks, and it was reported that the little ladies who gathered there were sewing with might and main.

"By heck, it 'pears to me that there is somethin' mighty queer goin' on 'round here," remarked Grandpa as he shuffled into the Chinaman's laundry one afternoon. "Such carryin's on I haven't seen for a long time."

"Allee same muchee slecrets," said the Chinaman, putting down his tiny iron and pushing out a chair for his visitor.

"Secrets!" shouted the old man. "Why, bless my soul, the air is full of 'em, and I reckon it's some of those new fangled ideas of the Lady of Fashion; she's always up to somethin' or t'other."

"Allee same we fine out if we wait long enough," laughed the Chinaman.

"Well, I 'spect you're right," growled Grandpa, "but we never did have any carryin's on like that when I was a youngster."

It wasn't long before all the Teenie Weenies knew what the secret was, for one morning they each received a tiny invitation written neatly in the dainty hand of the Lady of Fashion.

It was a very formal invitation to a grand ball in the cellar of a certain house.

There was much excitement among some of the little men, for it was whispered about that those who attended the ball were supposed to wear full dress suits and several of the little chaps had none. However, the Old Soldier, who was quite a good tailor, came to their rescue and everybody was provided with a dress suit, or "fish and soup suit," as Grandpa called them.

The ball was to be the most fashionable thing that ever had been given in Teenie Weenie land, and all the little folks could hardly wait for the appointed day.

The ball was to be given on the head of a drum which lay in a cellar not far from the shoe house. A paper box, which was found in the cellar, was pulled up beside the drum. Onto it steps were built up to the head of the drum. By cutting a door in the box it made a wonderful place for the little guests to leave their wraps, and a curtain, strung across the center of the box, gave the little ladies a snug place to powder their tiny noses. The head of the drum made a fine dance floor, and around the edges comfortable seats were placed.

It took quite a lot of argument to get the Dunce and Gogo to act as footmen, for they wanted to wear dress suits like the rest, but when they found out that they were to help the Cook serve the ice cream they were very willing.

The day of the ball the excited Teenie Weenies started to scrub and clean themselves many hours before the time set for the party, and a cleaner set of little folks never was seen.

At 9 o'clock the guests began to arrive and they were received at the top of the stairs by the Lady of Fashion and the General. Great candles flooded the place with light, and the Old Soldier, Paddy Pinn, and the Cowboy furnished music for the dancing.

At first the guests were rather stiff and formal, but the Dunce relieved the situation by falling down stairs with a tray full of dishes. The little people laughed right out loud when they saw the Dunce wasn't hurt, and from that moment on every one enjoyed themselves as they never had before.

A wonderful lunch was prepared by the Cook, and the footmen passed around dainty sandwiches, cocoa, lemonade, and ice cream.

All the Teenie Weenies attended the ball, except Grandpa, who stayed home and took care of the Lover Twins, and everyone said that the ball was the greatest event that had ever taken place in the Teenie Weenie social world.

"We had a wonderfully fine time, Grandpa," cried the Doctor when the little folks returned from the ball.

"And we had awful good things to eat," announced the Dunce. "See, I've brought some home for you," and the little fellow uncovered a tiny dish filled with ice cream.

"Once I went to a party," said Grandpa, dipping into the ice cream. "It was along in March in forty-nine—" But the little folks were too tired to listen to the story and they trudged off to bed, leaving the old gentleman to finish his ice cream and story by himself.

A MOST UNLUCKY MOUSE

"WELL," yawned Mr. Mouse, rolling off his soft cotton bed, "I think I'd better go out and see what I can find for breakfast; we haven't a bit of cheese or bread in the house."

"Now do be careful, dear," warned Mrs. Mouse, "and please don't go near that nasty old trap under the steps."

"All right, I'll be careful," laughed her husband and he hurried down the long hall which connected their home with a large cellar where all sorts of good things could usually be found. But on this particular morning Mr. Mouse found food very scarce and he was forced to climb about in many places in search of breakfast. While walking along the edge of a basket he chanced to see some crumbs of bread on the steps near by, and wishing to make a short cut he decided to leap onto an empty fruit jar that stood near, and from there onto the steps. He made a mighty leap onto the jar, but before he could balance himself he slipped and fell in.

His cries for help could not be heard, and it was some time before Mrs. Mouse, who had been alarmed at his absence, found the poor fellow.

"Oh, dear me! By the great cat's tail! This is most awful!" exclaimed Mrs. Mouse, bursting into tears.

"Go tell the Teenie Weenies!" shouted her husband. "They will come and help me out."

Mrs. Mouse ran over to the shoe house, and climbing up the front steps she rapped so hard that she scratched half the paint off the tiny door. Between bursts of tears Mrs. Mouse told the Teenie Weenies about her husband and the little people promised at once to help.

"Dear Mrs. Mouse," said the Lady of Fashion, trying to comfort the tearful mouse, "you must calm yourself. You must try to be calm."

"Great cat's claws!" exclaimed Mrs. Mouse, "I'd like to see you be calm with a husband in a fruit jar," and she burst into another fit of crying as she hurried back to her imprisoned husband, followed by the Teenie Weenies.

The Teenie Weenies quickly put up a ladder which they had brought with them, and the Doctor was soon lowered into the jar, where he found the poor mouse had two badly sprained legs. The General ordered the big windlass brought up, and when a derrick had been built on top of the fruit jar out of three strong clothespins the injured mouse was bundled into the biggest teenie weenie tablecloth and pulled out.

As it was late the Teenie Weenies decided to make the poor mouse as comfortable as possible, for it was quite a long way to the mouse's home, and they thought that after a night's rest he could stand the trip with less pain.

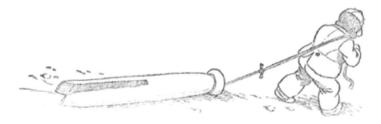

The little men made him a soft bed under the cellar stairs, and after he had eaten a Welsh rarebit, which the Cook brought to him, he fell into a sound sleep with Mrs. Mouse sitting watchfully by his side.

"We'll be over early in the morning and take your husband home," said the General, and the Teenie Weenies started back to the shoe house, for it was fast growing dark.

MRS. MOUSE ASKS A FAVOR

IT WAS quite late when the Teenie Weenies arrived at the shoe house, and it was almost nine o'clock when the little people had finished their supper.

"Well, we'd better all get to bed," said the General, pushing his chair back from the table, "for we have got to be out bright and early in the morning and take Mr. Mouse back to his home."

Gogo and the Turk helped the Cook wash up the supper dishes, and half an hour later every single Teenie Weenie was sleeping peacefully in his teenie weenie bed.

The Teenie Weenies had been asleep only a short time when they were awakened by a loud squeaking and scratching at the front door.

"Who dat?" cried Gogo, putting his head out one of the tiny windows.

"Its me," answered Mrs. Mouse. "Oh dear me."

"What's the trouble?" asked the General, joining Gogo at the window.

"Oh gracious me," wailed Mrs. Mouse, "I'm scared half out of my senses, for I'm afraid that old cat that lives next door might get in the cellar, and to think what would happen to my poor crippled husband just frightens me half out of my wits."

"We'll not desert you, madam," said the General kindly. "We'll come over immediately and take your husband home."

The Teenie Weenies soon dressed themselves, and Gogo hurried over to the hospital to call the Doctor.

"Hadn't we better take along one of the wagons?" asked the General, when the Teenie Weenie physician arrived.

"A wagon wouldn't do," answered the Doctor. "We could never take Mr. Mouse home in a wagon. Why, it would jar the poor mouse's injured legs until he couldn't stand the pain."

"Great grief!" cried the General, "how in the name of ripe cherries are we going to move him?"

"Very simple matter," said the Doctor. "We can carry him in a hammock, which we can make out of a sheet or tablecloth. This can be hung on a pole and we can carry him on our shoulders."

"I know where there's a pole that will be just the thing," shouted the Turk. "Come on, Gogo, and we'll get it."

The two Teenie Weenies hurried away in the darkness and presently they returned with a long handled paint brush.

The Cook brought out an old tablecloth and the little men set out for the cellar where the poor mouse lay.

It was dark, but the little fellows found their way without trouble, for Teenie Weenies can see almost as well as owls in the dark and in a short time they arrived safe and sound.

The injured mouse was soon put into the tablecloth and the ends were made fast to the brush handle. Six of the strongest Teenie Weenies were chosen to carry the mouse and they gently lifted the brush handle to their shoulders. The Teenie Weenies moved off carefully towards the mouse's home, which lay at the far end of the cellar.

The Dunce walked at the side of the hammock and carried the mouse's long tail over his shoulder, in order to keep it from dragging on the floor, for the poor fellow's spirits were mighty low and his tail would drag.

The mouse was carried through a hole in a brick wall, which was the entrance to his home, and laid gently on a bed of soft cotton. The Lady of Fashion helped Mrs. Mouse nurse her husband back to health and the Doctor called almost every day, while the Cook made all sorts of dainty dishes for the invalid.

THE SCOTCHMAN GOES SOUTH

THE Doctor had been very busy for some time. First the mouse, who had fallen into the fruit jar, needed a great deal of attention. The mouse lived quite a distance from the hospital and the Doctor called on him once a day for two weeks. Then a squirrel fell sick and the Doctor had to call on him for several days. The twins had the mumps and the Scotchman complained of the rheumatism.

The Scotchman's trouble caused the Doctor considerable thought. He worried over it for some time and then decided to take the matter up with the General. Taking his tall hat from its peg behind the office door he hurried over to the shoe house.

"General," he said as he stepped into the teenie weenie library and closed the door softly, "I'd like to speak to you for a few minutes."

"Go right ahead, Doc," said the General, throwing aside his work.

"It's about the Scotchman," said the Doctor, dropping into a teenie weenie rocking chair. "Scotty was troubled with rheumatism in his legs last winter, and the pain has started again this fall."

"It's all on account of his wearing those short kilt skirts, and going around in his bare knees," cried the General anxiously.

"Yes, I know it is," answered the Doctor. "I've tried to get him to wear trousers during the winter weather, but he will not do it. So, he's got to go south to spend the winter, where there's no cold weather, or he'll be sick."

"How in the world will he ever get down south?" asked the General.

"Oh, I've fixed that up all right," said the Doctor. "You know our friends, the birds, always go south for the winter?"

"Yes," nodded the General.

"Well, I was talking to a bird this morning, and she told me that she was starting south in a few days. I told her about our Scotchman, and she said that she would be glad to take him along. She said that he could ride on her back. She promised to look after him, and said she would bring him north again in the spring."

The General thought the plan a good one, and Scotty was told to pack his grip, and be ready to go by the end of the week.

The Teenie Weenies were greatly excited over the news. The Lady of Fashion mended all the Scotchman's clothes, and made him three tiny new shirts for the trip. The Chinaman washed everything he had that could be washed, starched and ironed his new shirts beautifully, and the others did all they could to make him comfortable and happy.

"Oh my," said the Dunce, when he heard the news, "I wish I had rheumatism, too, so I could go along."

The Teenie Weenies were up at the first break of day the morning that the Scotchman was to go. At the promised hour the bird flew up to the shoe house and lighted on the lawn.

"All aboard for Dixie," cried the bird, and the Teenie Weenies all swarmed out with the Scotchman among them.

"Here," shouted the Cook, running out with a big, neat package. "Here's your lunch. I put in all the things you like best."

"Jimminie," muttered the Dunce, as he hungrily watched the lunch being forced into the Scotchman's already overflowing grip, "I just do wish I was a-goin'!"

"We'll send your trunk to you by mail," shouted the Cowboy as the Scotchman climbed up on the back of the bird.

"All right," cried Scotty. "Thanks and good-by to everybody."

The bird spread her wings and gently rose from the ground. The Teenie Weenies stood shouting good-bys, and waving hands and handkerchiefs, till bird and Scotchman were lost to sight in the blue sky overhead.

FIRE! FIRE! FIRE!

"F-f-f-f-fire! F-f-f-fire!" shouted the excited Dunce, as he dashed up to the shoe house, gasping for breath.

"Where? What?" cried the General popping his head out of the front door.

"Over t-t-t-t-t-t-t-to th-th-th-th-th-th—"

"Great guns!" shouted the General, throwing up his hands in despair. "The house or whatever it is will burn down before you are able to tell us where the fire is. Out with it. Where is the fire? Quick!"

"It's it's over t-t-t-t-to th-th-th-th-the Lovers' house," gasped the Dunce, just as the Teenie Weenie fire engine and hook and ladder dashed up to the shoe house.

"To the Lovers' house," cried the General as he jumped onto the running board of the fire engine.

The little engine fairly flew over the melting snow and it nearly fell over as it skidded dangerously around a piece of paving brick which lay in its path. Presently the fire department arrived at the Lovers' bungalow, where they found clouds of smoke pouring out of the cracks around the back door and kitchen windows.

As Mr. and Mrs. Lover had locked up and gone with the Doctor to visit a sick mouse near by, it was found necessary to break in the back door, and soon a stream of water was thrown into the smoky kitchen.

The Chinaman was ironing one of the General's shirts when he heard the news of the fire, and in the excitement he ran over to the Lovers house, carrying the hot iron he had been using at the time.

The excited Dunce climbed up onto the roof, and if it hadn't been for Gogo he would have chopped a hole through the roof.

"What you-all goin' to do with dat ax?" asked the little colored lad as he watched the Dunce hurry up the ladder.

"Gonna chop a hole in the roof," answered the Dunce. "You've always got to do that; they always chop a hole in the roof when there's a fire."

"But there is no fire in the roof," cried Gogo. "It's down in the kitchen."

"Makes no difference," said the Dunce; "you always have to chop a hole in the roof." And if Gogo hadn't grabbed the ax from the Dunce's hand the foolish fellow would have done a lot of damage with it.

Almost a teacupful of water was thrown into the tiny kitchen and it did more damage than the fire, for really all that burned was a bean, which Mrs. Lover had put on the stove to cook, and which had boiled dry.

THE DUNCE TAKES A TUMBLE

"CRICKETY!" exclaimed the Dunce as he dropped into a chair before the Teenie Weenie fireplace. "Since the Scotchman left it's as dull around here as a lady's pocket knife," and the little fellow blinked mournfully into the fire.

"What's wrong, Dunce?" asked the Lady of Fashion, looking up from her sewing.

"Ah, I want to take a walk or somethin' and everybody is busy or somethin'."

"Why don't you get Gogo to go along? He always likes to take a walk," smiled the little lady.

"Ah, he an' the Cowboy an' the Turk are buildin' a fly trap over at the tool house. The Sailor and the Indian are helpin' the Cook get a spoiled potato out of the cellar. Paddy Pinn, the Doctor, the General and the Old Soldier are havin' a meetin' at the hospital and the Clown and the Poet are out in the back yard talkin' nonsense with a sparrow," growled the Dunce.

"I'd love to take a walk today, but I promised to mend this dress for Mrs. Lover and it has to be finished by four o'clock, as she and Mr. Lover and the Twins are invited over to the squirrel's house for dinner. Why don't you go over to the laundry and try Chuck and Zip? Maybe one of them would like to take a walk."

"Chink!" shouted the Dunce, "I never thought about the Chinaman and Zip," and jumping up he hurried over to the old tea pot, where he found Zip toasting his shins before the fire.

The Chinaman had just gone over to the hospital to deliver some shirts to the Doctor, but Zip was ready for a walk, and in a few minutes he slipped on his sweater and the two Teenie Weenies set off together.

There was one place the Teenie Weenies loved to visit best of all and that was any big house where big people lived, for there were always so many big and wonderful things to see.

The two little fellows made their way straight to the nearest big house, and crawling under the door they began to investigate the place.

"Let's crawl up on that," said the Dunce, pointing to a shelf high above their heads, "and maybe we can find somethin' good to eat."

After a hard climb the two Teenie Weenies landed on the shelf, but they found nothing but glass fruit jars, which towered above their heads.

"S-S-S-Say, Zip!" said the Dunce as he nodded his head in the direction of one of the jars, "that jar hasn't got any top on it and there are pickled peaches in it. I've just been thinkin' that we could get up on the shelf above and you could hold a string while I slid down into the jar and got some of the fruit."

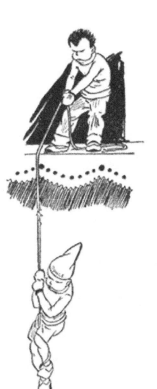

After a long hunt the two Teenie Weenies found a piece of string, and climbing up to the shelf the Dunce started to slide down into the jar. He got nearly half way down when the string snapped and the little chap dropped with a loud splash into the juice.

Poor Zip was scared half out of his wits and ran off for help as fast as his legs would carry him. He found three of the Teenie Weenies in the tool house, and grabbing up a piece of rope they followed the little fellow at top speed.

When they climbed up onto the shelf they all burst out with laughter, for the Dunce was a funny sight, standing on a pickled peach with the juice dripping off the end of his nose.

The Cowboy threw a rope to the Dunce and the rest of the Teenie Weenies soon pulled him to safety.

"S-S-S-Say," gasped the Dunce, rubbing the

juice out of his eyes, "don't t-t-t-tell the General. He'd give me an awful scolding for getting into this mess."

"Well, you know that it's not right to go meddling into things," said the Cowboy, "but if you promise not to try anything like this again, we'll not tell on you."

"I'll promise," answered the Dunce, "bu-bu-bu-but look at my clothes, they are spoiled."

"Me fix that all right," cried Zip. "Me take you to laundry and wash clothes for you."

Taking a roundabout way so they would not be seen, the Dunce and Zip soon reached the laundry, where the Dunce stripped to the skin and crawled into the Chinaman's bed, while Zip washed and dried the soiled clothes.

"They still smell a little of the pickled peaches," said the Dunce, as he put on his clothes.

"Your clothes not smell much like peach," said Zip, sniffing at the

Dunce. "Nobody notice him."

As it was nearly supper time, the Dunce hurried over to the shoe house, and when he drew his chair up to the tiny dinner table the Lady of Fashion looked suspiciously at him.

"Something smells funny," remarked the little lady.

"Smells sort of like pickled peaches," chuckled the Cowboy, winking at the Turk.

The poor Dunce turned as red as a cranberry and he was most uncomfortable for a few minutes, but fortunately the talk turned to other matters and he felt very much relieved.

While he ate his supper the Dunce made up his mind that he would never enter another pickle jar and to his credit let it be said that he has strictly kept his word.

THE CLOWN FALLS OFF A SPOOL AND KNOCKS DOWN A HOUSE

AFTER his experience in the pickle jar the Dunce made a resolution to try to be good whenever he went into a big house. But the busy little fellow couldn't keep out of mischief, and it wasn't long before he got into trouble again. He didn't really mean to be naughty, for he was a most kind hearted little chap, but being so full of life and so curious he simply couldn't be quiet.

He loved to look into everything he saw, and being a good climber he wanted to crawl over everything. The little people had been skating all morning and they had stopped at a house, on their way home, to warm themselves. The Dunce had gone prowling about the place and had found a child's play room with many wonderful toys in it which he wished his friends to see.

"Jimminie Christmas!" he shouted, "there's building blocks and dolls, chairs and tables and everything! Come on in!"

The Teenie Weenies followed the Dunce to a nursery where they found all sorts of pretty toys. The little folks enjoyed themselves for some time looking at the many playthings, but the thing they liked most was a beautiful arch or house made out of building blocks.

Of course, the Dunce had to climb to the very top of the house, where he sat shouting at the Teenie Weenies below.

"Jinks!" he cried, "you get a dandy view up here; I can see way over to the other side of the room."

"You'd better come down," warned the Doctor. "The first thing you know you'll fall off and break your foolish neck."

At this moment the Clown, who had been balancing himself on a spool, suddenly slipped and went crashing into the house.

"Run for your lives!" screamed the Cook, as the house toppled forward. One of the small boys, who had started to climb up the house, clung screaming to the column and the Dunce gave a mighty leap off the top, while those who were on the floor ran with all their might.

The house came crashing down and it was the luckiest thing in the world that no one was badly hurt. Outside of being badly scared and pretty well shaken up the small boy and Dunce were none the worse for their fall.

"This is a fine pickle," said the General. "Now we'll have to get pulleys and ropes and build this house up again just as we found it."

The Teenie Weenies hurried home for the necessary tools and it took fully four hours of hard work to build the house again just as they had found it. The little folks did the work so well that the child who had first built the house never suspected for a moment what had happened to it.

That night Rufus Rhyme wrote a verse about the Dunce's fall. It was called "Humpty Dumpty Dunce," and here it is just as the Poet set it down:

Twenty times a day or more, the Dunce goes tumbling on the floor,
He must be made of iron and rocks to stand so many bumpy knocks.

THE ARMY IS PUT TO ROUT

THE old derby hat which the Teenie Weenies used as a school house was also used as an armory. The second floor was given over to the army and here the little soldiers drilled every Wednesday night.

Their tiny guns and uniforms were kept in little cases which stood around the room. The uniforms were spotless and the tiny guns shone as bright as the new moon.

About four times a year the General ordered the army out for a practice march. "It toughens the men up and makes better soldiers out of them," he said, and most of the little soldiers seemed to like the experience.

One morning a tiny paper was pasted on the bulletin board and this is what it said, just as it was written by the General:

SPECIAL NOTICE
Thursday morning at eight o'clock every
enrolled member of the army will meet at the
armory for a practice march to the big woods
and back.
The General,
Commander in chief of the
Teenie Weenie army.

"Ah, crickety!" growled the Dunce, when he had read the notice. "It's too cold to go marchin' around in the snow."

"It won't hurt you any," said Paddy Pinn, who was standing near. "It's good for you—that's what it is—it's good for you."

"It may be good for me all right," answered the Dunce, "but it would be much better for me to be sittin' in front of the fire in weather like this."

On Thursday morning the little men gathered at the armory promptly at eight o'clock and when they had slipped into their uniforms the General stepped onto a little platform, at one side of the room, and made a speech.

"Men," he began, "while we get a great deal of good drilling in the armory once a week, it is quite necessary for us to get out of doors occasionally. We need the long marches to keep the army in good shape, for we never know just when it may be necessary to tackle a hard task and it is very wise to be prepared."

The soldiers formed in line in front of the school house and when the command was given the little army swung off, led by the General, who looked every inch a commander, sitting astride a big gray mouse.

As the little army trudged along through the snow they were suddenly thrown into a panic by the unexpected appearance of a huge rabbit, who popped into view over a snow bank directly in their path.

The appearance of the rabbit was so sudden the little army were frightened half out of their wits, and most of the soldiers turned and ran, in spite of the commands of the Old Soldier.

The mouse, on which the General rode, reared up on his hind feet, and the General was tumbled off into the snow.

"Well! Well! This is rather unusual!" cried the rabbit. "This is the first time I ever saw anybody run away from me; I'm usually the one that runs."

The rabbits voice was so pleasant the Teenie Weenies felt quite sure he would not harm them and soon they were gathered all about the big fellow, feeling his soft fur and asking many questions.

"Great grief!" exploded the General, picking himself up and brushing the snow off his coat. "That's a fine way to come bouncing onto an army. You came on us so quietly and suddenly you gave us a great start."

"I have to go along quietly," said the rabbit. "I have to sneak around, for there are so many hunters and dogs, who are always on the lookout for us poor rabbits. This spring I had thirty-three sons and daughters and now—now I am a widower with only seventeen children. Only last night I had to call in old Doc. Woodchuck to take some shot out of my oldest boy's skin."

"Ah, Mr. Rabbit," cried the Poet, "your sad story has given me an idea for a verse. While you were talking to my friends here I have been scribbling and with your kind permission I'll recite what I've written."

"I would be delighted to hear it if it isn't too long," said the rabbit. "You see, I've got to always be on the jump; can't stay very long in one place."

"This verse is very short," said the Poet. "In fact, it is no longer than its name. It's called 'The Tale of a Rabbit.'"

"The rabbit's life is full of strife,
His days are short and few;
For dodging shot becomes his lot
From the cradle to the stew."

"A very truthful and beautiful piece of poetry," said the rabbit, brushing a tear from his furry cheek. "I hope you will excuse me now, for I must hurry home and call the roll and see whether any more of my children are missing."

The Teenie Weenie soldiers watched the rabbit hop away and then they fell into line and continued their march to the big woods.

Paddy Pinn and the Cook had gone ahead of the army with food for the soldiers. They drove one of the army wagons, which was pulled by a team of mice, and when the hungry little soldiers arrived they found a thimble full of hot soup and other good things to eat.

After the men had rested for a time they set out on the trip home, where they arrived safely, a tired but happy and rosy, cheeked army.

COUGHING SYRUP

"GENERAL," said the Doctor, walking into the Teenie Weenie sitting room where the General sat before the fireplace, "I need some help."

"What's the trouble, Doc? Has the Dunce been getting into trouble again?"

"No," answered the Doctor, "that bump he got the other day when he tumbled off the block house ought to keep him steady for a while," and the Doctor drew up a chair and sat down, while the General threw several matches onto the fire.

"What I wanted to tell you was this," continued the Doctor. "Several of the children have a bad cough and—"

"I knew it, I knew it," cried the Old Soldier. "I knew they'd get their feet wet. They were over in the garden yesterday, sliding on some ice in a saucer, and I told them that ice was dreadfully thin and it would break, and they'd slip in and get wet and catch their death of cold."

"You're right," said the Doctor, "they got their feet wet, caught bad colds, and I haven't a bit of cough syrup in the house."

"I know where there's some," cried the Clown, who had been listening to the conversation. "The Dunce and I were looking for some pills to use as bowling balls, and we saw a big bottle of cough syrup on the bathroom window sill of that house next door."

"We'll go over and get some for you, Doc," said the General. "It will do us good to have the exercise."

Glad of an excuse to get out, the Teenie Weenies were soon on their way after the cough syrup.

The window sill on which the bottle of syrup stood was very high, but the Clown and the Cowboy soon climbed to the top. Lowering a piece of thread that two Teenie Weenies had carried between them for just such use, they soon pulled the rest of the little people up beside them.

"Now," said the Turk, who had been examining the bottle of syrup, "four or five of you fellows get hold and tip the bottle, and I'll hold the spoon somebody has thoughtfully left beside it, while you pour out a dose."

"Goodness gracious," cried the Lady of Fashion, "we don't need a whole spoonful!"

"Well, it says on the bottle, one teaspoonful for children,'" said the Turk.

"So it does, so it does," cried the little lady, as she stood on her tip toes and carefully read the label on the bottle.

"You see I'm right, don't you?" asked the Turk. "The Doctor told me to read carefully what it said on the bottle, and to bring about three doses. It says one teaspoonful is a dose for children, so we'll take about three spoonfuls."

"But that does seem an awful lot of medicine," said the Lady of Fashion doubtfully.

"It makes no difference," announced the Turk, "I'm going according to directions."

The Teenie Weenies poured out three spoonfuls of the syrup, which filled half an English walnut shell.

"Mercy on us," cried the Doctor, when he saw the Teenie Weenies carrying the heavy load of syrup up the walk to the shoe house, "you don't bathe in cough syrup."

"Well," muttered the Turk, "I went according to directions."

"The directions are all right for big children," laughed the Doctor, "but ours are Teenie Weenie children."

"Oh, my," exclaimed the Turk. "I never thought of that!"

"Well we can put it away and keep it," said the Doctor, "for it's likely we'll need it again before the winter is over."

The Doctor took out enough of the syrup to give the children each several doses and the rest was put in the half of a large English walnut. It was then carried to the cellar, covered tightly and put away for future use.

Of course the Dunce had to get into trouble while the rest of the Teenie Weenies were getting the syrup.

He climbed to the top of a talcum powder box, which stood on the window sill, and when he tried to pull the Chinaman up the foolish fellow slipped and tumbled off. He nearly fell on top of Zip, but that little chap managed to get safely out of the way.

The Dunce was badly shaken up by the fall and he almost knocked out one of his teenie weenie teeth.

"That's the last time I'll ever try climbing onto a talcum powder box," he said as he felt the tooth which had been bumped. "They're so awful slippery."

THE CLOWN HAS A NARROW ESCAPE

"WELL, we're goin' to have a change in the weather," announced Grandpa, as he peered out the tiny sitting room window at the sky.

"What makes you think so?" asked the Turk, who was playing checkers with the Cook.

"That toe of mine is hurting," answered the old man, "and that's a sure sign there's going to be a change," and with this prophecy Grandpa shuffled upstairs to bed.

Grandpa was quite right about the change in the weather, for it grew cold in the night, and the Lady of Fashion, who had to get up about midnight to give several of the children their cough syrup, noticed that the snow was falling.

In the morning the ground was covered with almost an inch of soft white snow and the little people shivered as they slipped on their tiny clothes.

After breakfast, several of the Teenie Weenies went out to play in the snow, but most of the little people were contented to sit before the warm fire.

"This snow storm reminds me of an experience of mine in forty-nine," said Grandpa, who pulled his chair so near the fire he almost scorched his shins. "I was cuttin' up an old ruler for fire wood one afternoon, when—"

"HELP! HELP!" screamed a voice from the outside.

"What's that?" cried the General, jumping to his feet.

Suddenly the front door burst open, and a frightened Teenie Weenie boy sprang into the room.

"Quick—help," panted the small boy. "The Clown has broken through the ice, and—and he—he can't get out! Quick—help!"

"Land sakes," cried the General, "where's the Clown!"

"He's over in the chicken yard, in a pan of wa-water," gasped the small boy.

With all speed the Teenie Weenies made their way to the chicken yard. As they hurried up to the pan they could hear the Clown faintly crying for help. The Turk and the Cook boosted the Sailor up to the top of the pan, where he caught on, and pulled himself over the edge. The poor Clown's head was only just out of the water, and he was holding fast to the edge of the ice.

"Throw me a board or a match, or something strong," shouted the Sailor to the others, waiting below. At once the little people began to dig about in the snow for the desired board.

"Oh dear," cried the Dunce, "if we only had a straw! I've always heard that a drowning man catches at a straw!"

"Here," shouted the Old Soldier. "Here's a burnt match, but it's frozen to the ground!"

The Turk grabbed the match and with a mighty heave he pulled it free and threw it up to the waiting Sailor. The Sailor carefully pushed the match out across the hole, and with its help he soon pulled the half frozen Clown from the water.

The poor fellow was carried quickly to the shoe house, where he was given a hot bath, wrapped up in a warm comforter and set before the fireplace. The Cook made cocoa for the Clown and brought it to him steaming hot.

"J-J-J-Jimminie f-f-f-fishhooks," stuttered the Dunce, as he watched the Clown sip the delicious cocoa, "I-I-I-I wish I'd have fallen into the pan so I could get some of that good cocoa."

"You don't need to fall into a pan to get some," laughed the kind hearted little Cook, "I'll bring you some," and in a few seconds he handed the Dunce a steaming cup.

"Crickety, but this is good," cried the Dunce, as he sat down beside the Clown. "J-J-J-Jimminie, I'm glad you fell into that pan."

"So am I," answered the Clown, as he drained his cup.

"Now I want you to tell me how this happened," said the General when the Clown had finished his cocoa.

"Why, a couple of us were skating," said the Clown, "and all at once the ice cracked, and—and I fell in!"

"Now then, I don't want to hear of any more skating in pans," said the General, shaking his finger at the open-mouthed Teenie Weenies, standing about.

"Yes, sir," several meekly answered.

"That is," continued the General, "unless they are shallow pie pans out of which you could wade. Remember!"

"We will," promised the little people.

A SQUIRREL TO THE RESCUE

THE weather continued cold for several days and the Teenie Weenies enjoyed almost a solid week of skating. An old dripping pan, which stood under a water spout at the corner of a big house near by, made a wonderful place to try out their tiny skates.

The ice was fully an inch thick, and as it was frozen solid it made a safe place to skate. The little people had a fine time on the smooth ice, but at the end of the week a thaw set in and they were forced to walk for their exercise.

"I'd advise you people to all go out and take a long walk, for I'm going to have a dandy dinner and I want you to have good appetites so you'll enjoy it," said the Cook Sunday morning as he stood tying on his apron in the Teenie Weenie dining room door.

"Wh-Wh-Wh-What are you going to-to-to have for dinner?" asked the Dunce. "A baked prune?"

"Well, here's the menu," grinned the Cook. "Potato soup, planked minnow, mashed peas and grape salad. For dessert we'll have a date stuffed with chopped nuts and whipped cream."

"Oh, good, good!" shouted the Dunce, catching the Lady of Fashion around the waist and dancing about the room.

In a few minutes the Teenie Weenies bundled themselves into their warm muffs, sweaters and mittens and started out on a long walk.

"Let's go down and see if the creek is frozen over," said the General. "I haven't been down that way for a long time, and it will make a nice walk for us."

There was quite a lot of snow on the ground, but as it was rather solid the little people were able to walk on it without much trouble, and in a short time they stood on the bank of the creek. For some time the Teenie Weenies stood watching the huge cakes of ice as they floated down the stream. In order to get a better view, the Lady of Fashion and the Doctor stepped out on a piece of ice which had not been broken away from the bank, and, to the horror of the little people, the piece of ice on which they stood snapped off and floated out into the surging stream.

It was impossible to swim among the sharp cakes of ice, as a Teenie Weenie would have been ground to pieces, for some of the cakes of ice were as big as soda crackers.

"Oh, jimminie crickets!" cried the frightened Dunce. "The Lady of Fashion and the Doctor will be drowned and then they won't get any of that go-go-good dinner the Cook is getting ready for us," and the poor Dunce burst into tears.

"Hold on a minute, Doc!" shouted a voice, and to the astonishment of the frightened Teenie Weenies a squirrel ran up a bush which hung over the stream. Hanging by his front feet, the squirrel swung his body down over the stream so that his bushy tail was only an inch or two from the water, and as the Lady of Fashion and the Doctor floated by he yelled to the Doctor to catch on.

Catching the Lady of Fashion about the waist, the Doctor grabbed the tail and the squirrel quickly pulled the two Teenie Weenies up to the bush, down which they safely crawled to the bank.

The Teenie Weenies were not the only ones who enjoyed a good dinner that day, for the little people presented the squirrel and his wife with four hickory nuts, five English walnuts, and a half dozen almonds for his bravery in rescuing the Lady of Fashion and the Doctor.

A CHRISTMAS PRESENT

ON CHRISTMAS morning the Dunce was first to jump out of bed. While he was getting into his teenie weenie clothes he happened to glance out of the tiny window.

"G-G-G-G-Great c-c-c-cat f-f-f-fish!" he yelled, and his eyes nearly popped out of his head, for on the walk before the school house stood a huge box.

"Get up, J-J-Jerry," cried the Dunce, pulling the bed clothes from the sleeping Clown. "There's a C-C-C-Christmas p-p-p-present out in the front yard and it's as big as, as, as a—jimminie—it's as big as everything," and the Dunce dashed out of the house at top speed.

All the little folks had been awakened by the noisy Dunce and in a few minutes they came pouring out of the shoe house like a stream of water.

"It's got a stamp on it and everything," shouted the excited Dunce, who had crawled up onto the box. "It's addressed to us too. The mail man must have left it. Hooray!" and the Dunce danced in such a comical way that all the little folks nearly burst from laughing.

Some kind person had sent the little people a pound box of candy and they were too excited to eat their breakfast, so the General told them they could open the box at once.

It took a great deal of labor for the little folks to cut away the paper and remove the box cover.

"Oh WHILLIKER!" howled the Dunce when the cover had been removed, "it's full of chocolates and bon bons, and great cats' eyes, there's a stick of peppermint candy."

"I don't know where in the world we're going to store all this candy," said the General. "There's enough to last us a year."

"You can store it in my bed room," cried the Dunce, "only leave just enough room for me to sleep in!"

"You mean, leave enough room so you can eat yourself to death," laughed the Cowboy.

"We can put a little of it in the cellar," said the Cook. "Maybe two or three pieces."

"There's room for four or five pieces in the tool house," suggested the Old Soldier, "and I think we can put the rest in the upper floor of the school house."

It was decided to store as much as possible in the school house and the little men began carrying the candy in as fast as they could.

"We can't put any more in here," shouted the Old Soldier, who came running out of the school house after several pieces had been stored away. "We've stored eight chocolates and a stick of peppermint upstairs and the beams have begun to bend. The floor will come tumbling down if we put another piece up there."

Other places had to be found to store the candy and when the last piece had been put away there wasn't a bit of vacant space left anywhere in the little houses under the rose bush.

"Great grief!" exclaimed the General, when the last piece had been tucked away, "we'll have enough candy to last us the rest of our natural lives."

"Don't you worry about that, General," cried the Dunce. "I can eat a whole chocolate myself."

After the Teenie Weenies had eaten their Christmas dinner, a whole chocolate was placed on the table and every one of the little people was allowed to eat all the candy he wanted.

The Dunce ate himself sick, but the next morning he was ready for more and the General made up his mind that the candy would not last as long as he first thought it would.

Several of the candies were stuffed with nuts and these the Teenie Weenies gave to their friend the squirrel, but most of it they kept for themselves and several pieces are still stored, this very minute, in the little houses under the rose bush.

MOTHER BUNCH DRINKS A TOAST

"WELL my toe is on the rampage again," announced Grandpa, several evenings after the rescue of the Doctor and the Lady of Fashion. "Whenever that old toe gets to hurtin', just look out for a change in the weather. It'll be mighty cold tomorrow or I'm no weather prophet."

"I hope it gets cold enough to freeze the ice again. That's what I do," cried Paddy Pinn, who was fond of skating, and had some new racing skates that he was anxious to try.

"I remember once in forty-nine," said Grandpa, "when the ice was frozen about six inches deep. I had to—" But he got no further with his story, for the Teenie Weenies started upstairs to bed and the old gentleman soon followed their example.

The next morning the weather was very cold and the Teenie Weenies were quite happy to stay indoors where it was warm and comfortable.

The Chinaman was braver than the rest, for that little chap wrapped himself up good and warm and set out to visit a mouse that lived near the rosebush.

"Hey, there, you Chinaman!" shouted a voice, as the little fellow hurried past a chicken yard.

The Chinaman glanced up at a huge chicken head that smiled down at him through the slats on the fence, and taking off his hat he made a very polite bow.

"Glood mornings," said the little chap. "It muchee clold mornings."

"Cold!" exclaimed the old hen, "I should say it was! I feel just like a feathered icicle and I wish I had a pair of nice warm felt boots for my feet—they're as cold as a doorknob."

"Allee same me muchee sorry and me will give you me muffler," said the little fellow, unwinding the tiny scarf from about his neck.

"I'm much obliged, I'm much obliged, but, whistling gizzard, that little muffler of yours wouldn't keep my little toe nail warm," laughed the old hen. "However, there is something you can do for me which would help me a great deal."

"Allee same you tell me and me be muchee glad to help," cried the Chinaman.

"Well," said Mother Bunch, for that was the old hen's name, "I'm as dry as a Saratoga chip. I haven't had a drink for three days. There's a pan of water in my coop, but it's froze. I beg your pardon, I mean frozen. I've pecked at the ice with my bill until it's as sore as an ingrowing pin feather and I haven't made a dent in it."

"Allee same me tell Gleneral and he come up klick and chop hole in ice," shouted the Chinaman.

"That's the idea! That's the idea!" exclaimed the old hen. "You see the folks who feed me just throw the corn into the pen and they never look at the pan of water and of course they never suspect that it's frozen. I you'll tell the General to come over and cut a hole so I can get a drink you will be doing an old lady a great favor."

"Me tell'm klick," cried the Chinaman, and off he ran for the shoe house as fast as he could.

The Chinaman told his story to the General and a few minutes later a number of the little people were on their way to Mrs. Bunch's coop. The old hen saw the little people coming and she was so excited she sat down and laid an egg right before the Teenie Weenies.

In just a few minutes the little folks set about cutting a hole in the ice, and it was quite a hard task, for the water was frozen to the depth of one Teenie Weenie foot.

"Well, here's to your health," said Mother Bunch when the little men had chopped a hole through the ice, and dipping her big yellow beak into the cold water she filled her bill and raising her head she let it trickle down her throat.

The pan which held the old hen's water had a long handle and the Dunce thought it great fun to crawl up on the handle and slide down to the edge of the pan. He did this several times with great success, but finally failed to catch the edge of the pan and he slid off onto the ice, and dropped kersplash into the cold water.

He was dragged out by the Turk and was sent home in disgrace, to the great amusement of the old hen.

Mrs. Bunch presented the egg she laid to the Teenie Weenies for their kindness, and the little people went home, happy to have such a friendly neighbor.

Made in United States
North Haven, CT
08 November 2023

43758708R00061